TWO BROTHERS

TWO BROTHERS

By: Joshua Savage

Cover, cover art, and interior design by:
BDDesign – www.lulu.com/BDDesign

Library of Congress Control Number: 2008911561

ISBN: 978-0-578-00235-4

Printed in the United States of America via Lulu Press
(www.lulu.com)
Publisher: Joshua Savage

For my brother:

Let us hope that we will one day reach our goals and fulfill our dreams – the both of us, together.

I

The masking tape cut the room in two distinct, supposedly even halves, except my half was just a little bit bigger, hardly noticeable, and if my brother did notice, he couldn't do much about it anyway.

"Now this is my side right here, OK?" I said pointing to the larger part of the room. "That's your side there. I don't gotta ask permission to come on your side because you got the door to get out, but you gotta ask permission to come on mine 'cause there's nothing you need on my side. Got it?"

"Uh huh," Jeremy nodded with an innocent trademark mischievousness in his eyes. When we were in the same room he didn't dare set foot across the tape, but the second I left for any length of time he rummaged through everything he possibly could. He tried on my clothing, played with my toys - always ruining something in the process.

My brother and I were staying with grandmother again while our parents were off doing God knows what. At her house we shared a room, a situation that I despised, but I loved to stay with grandma nevertheless. She spoiled us with homemade candy and ice cream, bought new toys at the store and allowed us to watch MTV - just like a grandma should do. We deserved it or at least I did.

My brother was the troublemaker, always annoying and aggravating. I never understood why mother gave him birth, depriving me of my rightful place as an only child. Who says I needed a little brother to keep me company? My fantasy world of Star Wars and Spiderman filled the void of loneliness.

Once I attempted to sell Jeremy. Mother took the two of us shopping. An old security guard remarked how cute of a kid he was. I immediately tried to negotiate a price.

"I'll give 'em to ya for $20." Not realizing the seriousness of my offer, the man and mother laughed. She retold the story often.

Mother, a hardcore Christian, never allowed us to watch certain channels on television, so at grandma's I usually watched MTV or if I spent the night I tried to stay up late and watch Cinemax after dark. Too young to be with women, I still liked to see them naked. Call it childhood curiosity.

With one last warning I left the room while Jeremy still sat quietly on his side of the floor, watching me peculiarly. I peeked around the corner a few times to spy, but he was already engaged in some pointless activity of his own. His mind moved quickly.

I turned on the television and sat on the floor only inches away, another harmless childhood pleasure mother forbade, and watched music videos nonstop until Michael Jackson's '*Thriller*' lit up the screen. That was the video I had really wanted to see, the one that lasted fifteen minutes where M.J. turns into a werewolf and zombies dance in the street, everyone's favorite at the time.

About half way through the song a loud crack like something had broken in our room caught my attention. Though I did not want to miss a second of the video I raced to the room, sure Jeremy had committed some irreversible wrong. He quickly threw something under the bed then turned around attempting to look normal but instead appeared frightened.

"What'd you do?" I yelled shoving him out of the way and reaching under the bed.

"Nuthin." He suddenly ran from the room and out the door to grandmother tending her garden in the back yard. Under the bed lay a piece of a brand new toy, barely out of the box, a new Transformer that changed from a robot to a Ferrari. I reached and found another part and then another. I screamed a curse word and pursued Jeremy to the backyard.

"Mamaw, Josh is gonna hurt me!" He stood behind her frail bent figure while her old withered hands dug in the dirt, eyes never looking up.

"Josh, leave your brother alone. Don't hurt him now." She spoke with a soft and caring tone. I had never heard her raise her voice.

"He broke my new Transformer, the one you just got me." My hands reached around my grandmother attempting to grab him but he was well protected.

"Jeremy, why'd you do that?" She briefly glanced at him.

"I didn't mean to. I was just playing with it and it broke."

"You did it on purpose! You always do that to my stuff!"

"Calm down. We'll get you a new one when we go back to the store. I'm sure he didn't mean to." Unphased by our yelling, she shook the loose dirt from the roots of a tomato plant she was transplanting.

"He never means to!" I stomped back inside the house and attempted to fix my Transformer with no luck, another new toy ruined.

Pouting, I returned to the living room and watched TV. If I waited long enough Jeremy would forget my anger and allow himself to become vulnerable again. Grandmother returned inside, Jeremy lagging close behind, staring because he knew I was about to attack. I ignored him, didn't even bother to look up. Grandma took off her gloves and laid them near the sink, washing her hands with grandfather's soap, a strong soap made especially for people with greasy hands. His hands were the hands of a mechanic, permanently rough and cut up, filthy everyday upon coming home.

"What ya'll want for dinner," grandma asked. Laziness was definitely not a trait she possessed. To sit still was a sin. If she wasn't in the garden or cooking, she was sewing, cleaning, or reading those sappy romance novels that push the envelope between romance and porn.

Grandfather had his own version of relieving stress. Sometimes at night if I couldn't go to sleep I walked into the living room while he sat there alone, wearing only his underwear and an old worn out T-shirt with a pocket on the front to hold his generic cigarettes. I jumped on the couch next to him and glanced at the TV screen. The scrambled picture showed a tit or an ass here and there. I could tell it was the Playboy channel, but my grandparents didn't have a subscription to it. If I sat long enough he changed it, probably not really caring if I watched it or not, but not wanting me to say anything to mom or grandma. I never did.

"How 'bout some pizza or a hamburger?" my brother asked. He ate junk food like crazy and never had cavities. I brushed at least three times a day and had one almost every time I visited the dentist.

"How 'bout some fried chicken, then I'll make us a milkshake later on?" She cooked the best southern meals anyone could ask for, greasy and filling, with tea as sweet as candy. She always snuck in lima beans or other vegetable to make sure we ate something healthy but I didn't mind.

Minutes later she was in the kitchen banging pots and pans, the grease popping in the air and the smoke lingering through the house, the smell of southern cooked food strong in my nostrils. Jeremy stayed in the kitchen for a while but became bored and walked toward the living room slowly. His eyes watched me hoping I had forgotten his devious action. I ignored him, pretending to be glued to the TV. He situated himself on the smaller couch. Several minutes passed, and when I knew he was comfortable, I pounced on him, throwing punches to his legs and arms, spots less likely to leave marks. He cried for mercy.

"Mamaw, help!" I heard a pan drop and I jumped back to the other couch and lay still like nothing had happened. My brother whined and cried. Grandmother looked furious.

"Josh, what did you do? I can't leave you two alone for five minutes. Go to your room! Her wrinkles were more pronounced when she was angry.

"But I didn't do nuthin'. How come I get in trouble and he don't?"

"Yer too big to be beatin' up on him. You know better. Now go. You can come out when dinner's ready." She tried to be tough and stern but failed miserably. Still, I obeyed out of respect.

"Man, I always get in trouble. It's not fair."

I stomped into my room angry but satisfied. If my toy was broken at least I had a little satisfaction knowing my brother would be in pain for the next few days. I sat quietly trying to fix my Transformer. After a few minutes I figured out how to snap the pieces back into place. It wasn't broken after all. Of course I never told anybody. I got a brand new Transformer the next time we went to the store.

II

Jeremy watched with curiosity as I prepared the bird trap in the backyard. I found a sturdy stick, about six inches long, and used a special knot I learned in Boy Scouts to tie the string to it. The string was long enough to reach into the front yard where we could hide ourselves behind what was left of the riddled fence. A friend and I had felt like testing out our new boxing gloves on the already rotted boards one day. My parents had not given me an allowance since.

Pillaging through our rusty shed I found an empty cardboard box inside and propped it up with the stick.

"Hey, go inside the house and grab me some bread real quick." Jeremy ran inside excited to be helpful. He returned with a full loaf.

"I don't need all that!" I took a few pieces and crumbled them up under the box.

Behind the fence we waited and waited, birds landing on top of the box and on the fence above it. Every time one came close my heart began beating faster and faster, but none were foolish enough to venture under the trap. I wanted to catch a cardinal or a blue jay, colorful Southern birds. Sparrows were too dull and boring. They dominated the neighborhood, but the others, it wasn't as common to see them. Still, I would be happy to catch anything with my new trap.

After thirty minutes that seemed like hours, we decided to go eat lunch.

"You're making too much noise. That's why they aren't coming. They can hear you." Jeremy was always a good scapegoat when something went wrong.

"But I didn't say nothin'," he genuinely expressed.

"But you're movin' and stuff. They can hear that. Birds are smart. They got good ears."

"I'll be more quiet then."

Mother made us bologna shaped like Pac Man and the ghosts along with sliced apples and cheese. To drink we had milk. I liked milk but preferred Coke or Kool-Aid, which she allowed us to have only occasionally. We made up for it at grandma's.

At the kitchen table we watched our trap to see if the birds realized it was abandoned. Naturally, as soon as I put the first bite of food in my mouth a blue jay landed in the perfect spot to be captured. I swallowed without chewing and ran out the front door. Jeremy followed. Of course by the time we arrived to the fence the bird had flown away.

"Man, you ran out here too loud. Ya scared 'em off!" Obviously this was a ridiculous excuse but little brothers were made to put the blame on.

"Did not. You were louder than me," he said assuredly.

"Did too." I shoved him. "I'm goin' back inside to eat."

Upon entering the house mom said,

"Finish your lunch before ya'll go back out there. It's bad to eat in a rush. You know how many times you're supposed to chew your food? At least twenty. Those birds will be there when you get done."

"Jeremy made too much noise, mom," I tattled.

"Did not."

"Whatever. Maybe you should just stay inside when I go back out."

"Fine. I will." His feelings were mildly hurt.

"Josh, quit bein' mean to your brother." I heard this all the time.

After lunch I went back outside and took some fresh bait to lie out for the birds. It looked like they had eaten most of the bread under the trap for lunch about the same time I had eaten mine. Jeremy remained inside, peering out the back window. I didn't want him to interfere with my imminent success.

Another hour passed without luck. The birds taunted me by landing everywhere but under cardboard box where I could tug the string. I began getting bored and frustrated. I was determined to catch a bird one way or another. Once I caught it, I had no idea what I would do. Keep it as a pet? Poke at it until I got bored? My boyish curiosity wanted to catch one for the thrill.

I went back inside the house. Jeremy had lost interest in watching and focused on something else. In my room I had a Daisy BB rifle that I had gotten for Christmas the previous year. Since my trap failed to work, I would shoot a few birds just for target practice. With interest, Jeremy stood in the doorway.

"Whatcha gonna do now?" he asked.

"What does it look like? The trap don't work so I'm gonna shoot a couple of 'em."

"Can I try?" His eyes lit up.

"I guess. I'm gonna go first though."

"OK."

We returned to the backyard and searched for a good hiding spot. Our backyard was filled with all sorts of junk; a swing set, a huge tractor tire we used for a sand box, countless toys strewn around, a deep hole we dug hoping to find treasure, a rusty aluminum shed and an above ground swimming pool that stood about three feet high. We chose the swimming pool.

Not a minute later a sparrow landed on the fence in perfect view. I aimed and pulled the trigger. Feathers flew everywhere as the bird fell to the ground.

"No!" Jeremy shouted. He began crying and ran quickly into the house.

"I thought you wanted a turn. You can shoot next," I yelled after him, proud of the accuracy of my first shot. He had already gone inside the house. I didn't understand why he was so upset. Minutes earlier he seemed excited and wanted a turn to shoot.

The bird was completely motionless, a small sparrow. I picked up the stick from the trap and started poking to make sure it was dead. I didn't dare touch it for fear of getting some type of disease. Mother warned me how dirty birds were. I decided to let it sit there until maybe a cat or some other animal came along and ate it later.

Without Jeremy to watch me, I didn't want to shoot any more birds. Probably I had wanted just to show off anyway. I retreated into the house to find my brother sitting with his head in mother's lap still crying.

"Josh, why did you have to do that? You know better. That's not why we bought you the gun, to kill birds. You can be so mean sometimes. Now put the gun up and don't use it again without asking." Mom was rubbing his head as he peered at me through her arms like I was a monster. I felt as if I had committed a crime and went to jail in my room. I saw nothing wrong with what I had done. I was just being a curious kid. But nevertheless, I felt bad for scaring my brother or whatever I had done to him. I remained in my room until dinner, playing GIJoe and reading comic books.

III

"See the one and only Jeremy Savage, child prodigy, before he gets famous, only two dollars!" I yelled with enthusiasm as members of our family reentered grandma's house after I had asked them to briefly step outside while my brother and I prepared for the concert. Without question, they stepped into the warm spring evening, smoking and talking adult-talk.

The small dining room where Jeremy would soon play his first live show was limited, especially the seating. Years of collected antiques filled most spaces, and besides a tacky seventies-looking couch, there were only folding chairs and a flimsy piano bench I had snagged. A large black Baldwin piano occupied almost an entire wall, but everything else moveable we had temporarily stored in another room until after the show. Grandma made us promise to be careful with her things and return them to the exact spot where we found them.

Our family thought it funny that I charged them to get into their own home, but they still paid, humoring us in a typical parental manner. They seemed excited enough. Mother prepared her camera to take photos. She dressed up pretty, make up and hair done as if she were attending a real concert. She always spent time fixing herself up, often to the point where father became irritated.

"You're mother is going to be late to her own funeral," he complained, especially if we had to be somewhere. "But, that's how most women are. Just wait till you have a wife. You'll see."

It never bothered me much. In fact, I felt lucky mom was so pretty. Sometimes my friends even told me so. I was even happier when my parents weren't fighting which seemed less and less often as I grew older. Even when they were getting along, it appeared to be contrived, as if it were an appearance to ease our minds. A strong tension existed between them, ready to explode at any moment.

I was the entrepreneur of the family, Jeremy the musician. To prepare for the show I made a large, colorful sign with Jeremy's name and another with the prices of food and cold beverages that I took straight from grandma's fridge and pantry. While my brother played the show and wallowed in the attention, I would sit at the back and sell concessions to make extra money.

Suddenly Jeremy appeared from a door leading from the hall. He wore his newest pair of pants; beige, fake leather, and super-tight. His shirt mismatched perfectly and he wore a black pair of sunglasses a little too big for his face. His hair was slicked back, still wet with water. The smile on his face was contagious, infecting everyone in the room.

As he entered, the anticipant crowd stood and began to clap and cheer. Jeremy smoothly picked up his guitar and turned on the cassette player. Earlier, we had put together a mix tape, 'Chartbusters' we called it, with a mixture of our favorite bands. He planned to lip-sync and play the guitar to the songs. Even though he could play the guitar some already, he had not quite reached the level of the musicians on the cassette.

Then the music began. With the mannerisms of a true star, arrogant and attention loving, he began to strum his guitar and sing. His face changed expressions every time the music hit a different note. Like an actor on stage, he wooed the crowd, making eye contact with each individual to search for approval. My mother snapped picture after picture.

As I sat in the back, I glanced back and forth from my brother to the family. They were entranced, proud, and hopeful.

"Maybe one day he will be a famous musician," I thought. *"He has the heart and the desire. He has the energy and ambition. Maybe I can be his manager, handle the financial aspect of the rock business. We can make some serious money."*

After every other song, Jeremy pushed pause on the cassette player and disappeared to the back bedroom to change clothes. This afforded my parents time to go outside and smoke and gave me the opportunity to sell more refreshments. Truthfully, the thought of being a rock star enamored my brother more than actually being one. He craved the fame and attention. Everything else - the money, the girls, the music – they all came secondary.

The cassette tape eventually played completely through. The small crowd stood, clapped and whistled for an encore. After playing two extra songs from another tape the show was over and Jeremy had changed clothes at least five times. My mother had taken at least a full roll of film. The smokers had smoked several cigarettes. And I had sold all of grandma's cokes and most of her snacks. My brother and I split the profits. We decided to have another concert the next weekend we stayed grandma's house.

IV

Father's apartment smelled like a mixture of sweat and vodka, the cheap kind. People often said he drank like a fish. After years of arguing and threatening to leave, mother finally divorced him. Then, unexpectedly and contradictory to all who knew her, she fell off the deep end, went crazy, lost her mind. But it wasn't the divorce alone that caused the breakdown.

Around the same time her brother, my uncle, died in a tragic car accident while driving home from work late one evening. Already extremely upset and with everything seeming to happen at once, mother fell over the edge. She and my uncle were tight, probably as close as siblings could be. Countless times before he died she stressed the importance of being close to your family, especially a sibling.

"You need to treat your brother right, Josh." Her voice was calm and serious. "When it comes down to it, all you have is each other. After we're gone, there will just be the two of you." Every word came straight from her heart. For this reason I understood her pain when my uncle passed. Together everything transformed her from the perfect, Christian, make you eat your vegetables mother to an addict in only a few short years.

By now Jeremy and I attended a new school and lived with my drunken father in a cramped apartment. The courts agreed that even though an alcoholic, he was better fit to raise us. Besides, he didn't stay drunk everyday, probably not even a few days a week, but enough to be ineffective as a husband and a father.

If not for the new friends I had made in the apartment complex, I would have been utterly miserable. I played outside as much as possible. In the morning I woke up and left, came inside only for food, and then left again until dark. Many times we were the last kids to go inside at night, my brother and me. Nobody told us when to come home. My friends acted jealous but of course they never realized the true situation until they came over and saw him laid out on the couch.

"He's asleep," I often said. Some knew the truth. Others maybe not.

The constant chaos of our life brought my brother and me closer. I fought with him on a regular basis and he continued to break and ruin anything of mine he could get a hand on, but I lost the urge to get rid of him, though I never admitted to it. Times occurred when my parents fought badly and the only person I had around was Jeremy. We needed each other.

On a dreary afternoon father was passed out on the couch, not unusual, and mother stopped by to check on us. She raised hell after we tattled that father had picked us up from school and had driven us home drunk. The yelling that followed was loud enough for the entire apartment complex to hear. Nosy friends and neighbors began to walk towards the apartment and watch the drama that ensued.

Father woke up, his face red and sweating profusely, stumbling to and fro, his high blood pressure through the roof. The shouts had sobered him up enough to defend himself.

"You ain't no goddamn better, Jerrie! Why are the kids here right now if I can't take care of 'em? You sure as hell can't take care of 'em. Look at ya." He raised his voice slightly but rarely yelled. It was the taunting way he said things that got under mom's skin, condescending and arrogant.

"You'll end up killin' them is what's gonna happen!" Mom screamed furiously. By now several neighbors had surrounded the apartment. I yelled for my parents to stop, ashamed and embarrassed. My brother sat motionless on the curb outside among a small crowd looking scared, almost in tears.

Suddenly mom went to her orange Chevette and retrieved her purse, pulling out a pair of scissors. I thought for sure she was about to stab my father.

"Dammit, I bet you don't take those kids anywhere again today." With the most profound look of anger and hatred I had ever witnessed she ran towards father's brown S10 pickup and forcefully with all her strength jabbed the front tire with the scissors. The air hissed out like a snake and the rubber went flat immediately. She pulled the scissors out and made her way to the other side but not before father had lost his temper. The redness of his face was caused by anger instead of alcohol now. He raised his foot up while gripping both sides of the driver's side window on the Chevette and with all his might he kicked it in, the glass shattering and falling to the ground.

The crowd stood around amazed. They were witnessing a drama better than reality television. Mother ran towards father and began throwing wild punches as he held her arms the best he could to block the blows. She kicked and screamed.

"We've called the police!" someone finally

shouted. This wasn't the first time the police had come to settle a family argument. I had called them several times in the past. Not simply for shouting or arguing but when my parents took it to the next level - throwing things or becoming violent. Mom lost her temper easily and often. Father was a drunk but he was a passive drunk. It took him a lot to get going. Today was the perfect example.

Mother pulled away and walked towards her car staring at the damage. I ran to my room upstairs crying. After phoning grandmother and explaining everything that happened, she promised to pick us up right away. Meanwhile, I organized my comics to divert my mind.

My brother walked inside and sat at the bottom of the stairs. "Josh," he called in a timid manner, anxiety in his voice.

"Jeremy?" I called and walked to the edge of the stairs. He saw me crying and rushed up. I grabbed him and held on tight, the biggest hug I had ever given him. I refused to let go. At that moment he tried to be the stronger of the two of us.

"Everything will be OK Josh. We still got each other no matter what," he said calmly. When I looked into his eyes the anxiety had departed, replaced with a new strength in the words he had said to me.

"You're right. You're right. We got to stick together don't we?" I wiped my eyes.

"Yep." He smiled wide and ran back downstairs to get an update on what was happening. I felt better.

When the police arrived they said the same thing as usual. They warned my parents,

"The next time something like this happens we'll have to take ya'll both to jail. We don't want these kids to havta witness no more of this, got it?" They didn't want our young minds to be scarred anymore. Both parents blamed the other but the police were impartial and uncaring who was at fault. Probably they witnessed these types of incidents several times a day.

Grandmother arrived shortly afterwards. Immediately she added to the fire by blaming mother in front of everyone. The look on my mother's face went from one of anger to profound shock and helplessness as if she had been beaten. It was never my father's fault, not grandma's little baby boy.

The cops asked mother to leave and asked grandmother to take us home. Seeing mom in tears and obviously worried about us, I wanted nothing more than to console her. She had nobody to go home to, more depressed after the thrashing grandmother had given. When father was sober, grandmother would bring us back to the apartment and mom would still be alone at home, dejected and probably wallowing in self-pity.

I wanted to hide, to be alone, far away from every family member. I looked at my brother in the back seat. He smiled, still radiating from his earlier sense of superiority. He had comforted me. At that moment he was the stronger one. I felt terrible, weak, and powerless against the circumstances.

V

"Dammit! I'll never find it in here!" I ravaged through the impenetrable filth of my brother's room searching for a shirt I was sure he had taken. The floor was visible in few spots, dirty and clean clothes, magazines, food, and every other imaginable odd and end littered every corner of the room. To make it more uninhabitable the walls were painted black as a night without stars, done sloppily and hastily, with numerous uneven and torn posters adorning the walls.

"How did he get into my room this time?" I wondered while I opened the closet door only to find more of a mess. I could barely stand to be in the room for more than a few minutes at a time, the stench unbearable, the air thick and stuffy. Wait until Jeremy got home. I would kick his ass if he didn't tell me exactly where the shirt was. I would probably kick his ass anyway just for getting into my room again.

My bedroom door had a dead bolt lock, the only one in the house. Beside myself, only my stepmother had a key, a condition she set but promised not to enter without a justifiable reason. The lock protected my personal belongings, primarily from Jeremy. Sometimes it worked, but obviously not always.

Like our personalities, our rooms were the antithesis of each other, mine organized and meticulous, his disordered and chaotic. Every single object in my room was accounted for and placed in a specific spot; white socks separated from black, t-shirts from long sleeves and still further from button downs and sweatshirts, hardback books separated from soft covers, fiction from nonfiction, magazines ordered by month and year, not a single spot or stain on the floor, nothing out of place, orderly like a drill sergeant checked it thoroughly every morning. And so when something went missing, I knew exactly what it was. This in essence was my way of containing the turmoil that defined my life.

Jeremy's room represented a chaos that permeated every aspect of his life, on a collision course with destruction, that fateful end realized by everybody but discussed by no one, and more likely than not, made nothing more than an excuse for misguided behavior. Our minds viewed the world from two different realities, yet we comprised one soul, one brother not fully functional without the other. It would take us years to realize this unique and deeply profound bond we shared. Until that climatic time we would settle for the carefree and oblivious character of childhood.

Anxiously I waited for Jeremy to return home still wondering,

"How did he get into my room?" Time passed slowly, my mind thinking of nothing else, almost obsessed with a shirt, an object that to me represented a threat to my kingdom, my safety and security. Though I had a closet full of clothing, I was determined to wear that specific shirt, the almost new polo with navy blue and aqua stripes. Nothing else could be worn.

The front door swung open followed by two loud and obnoxious voices, that of my brother and his goofy friend, tall and lanky, wearing glasses but still squinting to see everything. Without warning I jumped over the couch and tackled my brother to the ground, not even asking him to admit guilt but assuming it without question, and let punches fly to every part of his body except his face. I didn't want to leave marks that would get me in trouble with my parents later. His friend sat back speechless and scared. He had witnessed these types of fights between us before.

After bringing tears to his eyes, I finally asked

about the shirt. For a minute I had forgotten the reason I was beating him in the first place.

"Where is my shirt? I know you got it." My fist reared back and was ready to strike again.

"I didn't get nuthin'. Let me go." I held him tightly to the ground knowing that the minute I let him go he would try to retaliate. He possessed a wild temper, uncontrollable when unleashed.

"The striped blue one, where's it at? I warned ya not to go in my room again."

"I didn't get it. Let me go."

Though I didn't believe him, I had no choice but to release him or stay in the same position. He never admitted to guilt and lied like a car salesman.

"I'm gonna let ya go but you got to promise not to do nuthin'. You hear me? Promise." His face was blood red, his teeth clenched.

"OK. Just let me go."

I jumped up and waited for a counter attack. He grunted sounds of rage while he wiped the tears from his face, snot running from his nose, wild eyes glaring at me. His friend had not budged an inch, still bewildered though he saw us fight frequently. He followed Jeremy to his room and seconds later they reappeared, Jeremy with a shiny object in his hand, a replica of a knight in armor, small but heavy and made of pure metal. Before I had time to think he reared back and threw it, nailing me right in the head.

The knight left his mark, drawing blood, but pain never sets in until the brain has time to stop and think after the immediate action which happened to be still in progress. I ran towards his room where he had shut and locked the door behind him. After the knight struck me, Jeremy's rage immediately turned to fear. He realized his actions would be punished by a further beating. Deep down we didn't really want to hurt each other, but never thought about the consequences until afterwards.

I kicked in the door breaking the hinges and attacked with punches, this time not distinguishing where they landed. He did his best to block them but my fury had been unleashed. For a good sixty seconds I lost control. Again his friend sat there squinting, dumbfounded and scared to intervene.

When I regained my senses, I stopped swinging and stood above him. I felt like a giant beating on a midget and stepped away, hoping he had learned his lesson. Instead he was only angrier and reached for a baseball bat. I fled to my room and locked the door.

The bat crashed into the wood with two or three loud attempts at busting the door open and then suddenly everything became quiet.

No way would we be able to cover up this fight. I didn't dare come out for hours until father and stepmother returned home from work. And when they did, we both felt the repercussions as they yelled and grounded us for the foreseeable future. Our fighting lasted minutes while their punishments lasted weeks. It was never worth it. Later I remembered that one of my friends had borrowed my shirt.

VI

Cold as ice the crystal-clear water of the river felt, nine million gallons an hour released by the natural springs, attempting to invalidate the damage we senselessly wrecked, yet ultimately losing the battle to offset the steady and progressive ruin we incited. The river became in its natural state filled with cans and bottles, plastic baggies, urine, and whatever else the hundreds of humans a week that canoed it lost on the ten-mile trek from the drop-off back to their campsites. Not that we were sober enough to realize our haphazard actions at the time nor were we coherent enough to feel the full effect of the water which upon contact brought up chill bumps on our skin and wiped out half of our buzz, causing us to consume significantly more alcohol than we were able to do at any other time.

We had a good lead now, Bubba and I, past my brother and his friend, who, when I looked back, were completely out of sight.

"Let's pull over here. This is a good spot." I said. The brown weathered pebbles formed a small bank, the perfect site to pull up the canoe. The numerous trees and overgrowth would hide us from view of others paddling down the river.

"He knows ya smoke. I don't know why ya try ta hide it so bad," Bubba said calmly grinning through his perfect white teeth because he thought it funny that I became so paranoid when I attempted to smoke around my brother. We jumped from the rented aluminum canoe with drenched shoes weighing about ten pounds more than normal and pulled it ashore. I glanced back one last time to make sure my brother was still far in the distance.

"Man, come on. I'm tellin' ya he knows. Ya should jus' lighten up an' smoke with 'em. I bet he's smoked 'fore anyways." Bubba was country, backwards in most people's sense of the word, but he still possessed a selective knowledge, a sort of manipulative understanding of human behavior. That and he could hunt and fish like nobody's business.

"Still man, I don't want him smokin' with me. It just don't feel right. He's not old enough." I realized the hypocrisy of what I said before Bubba repeated it.

"Man, what? You was smokin' in ninth grade. He ain't much younger."

What I failed to mention, what I couldn't mention

without sounding silly, was that I felt responsible for his actions. In a sense, I was a role model, the older brother. Jeremy looked up to me. Though the years of beating up on him had mostly passed, we were far from the level of being best friends.

We walked through the foliage until we reached an open space. Spring River was the best place in the world at that time in our lives. Only in high school, it gave us a chance to get away from our parents reign for a few days and live a little. The drive was close, about three hours from home, and our parents had no problem with us going most of the time, obviously not knowing the things we were doing or maybe knowing, but allowing us to have a little fun anyway.

The trip was the first time my parents allowed Jeremy to go with me. They trusted me to keep an eye on him. Smoking pot together probably wasn't what they had in mind and though I doubted he would tattle, I still didn't want to take chances.

Hidden from view of the river, Bubba took out a plastic baggie that contained his cigarettes along with a few joints and a lighter. He checked to make sure no water had leaked into the baggie and luckily it hadn't. Pulling out the fattest rolled joint, he joyfully lit the end and smiled,

"Yeah buddy. We fixin' ta be fucked up." He took a long puff until he coughed, and still choking handed it to me. "Man, that's some good shit right there boy."

No sooner had I took a hit myself than I heard movement in the bushes.

"What'll ya'll doin'?" Jeremy walked casually towards us with an evil grin, one that informed me the jig was up. His friend was close behind, smiling goofily.

"Nothing." I said surprised, fumbling and dropping the joint as I tried to pass it to Bubba. He picked it up quickly looking a little pissed, wiped it off, and took another hit, uncaring and indifferent to the fact that my brother had arrived. Jeremy appeared hurt because he knew I was lying.

"Nothin' huh?" He stood motionless except for his eyes that shifted between both me and the joint. Bubba laughed.

"Ha! Yer busted now buddy. May as well smoke with 'em." He handed the joint to Jeremy. I began to make a motion to say no but stopped short. I might as well let him. It would finally stop the endless secrecy that had been occurring for so long.

"I smoked before Josh," he said attempting to look like a professional. He took a long hard puff without coughing and held it in, tilting his head back and letting the smoke out slowly.

"I figured as much." I stood, arms folded in an uneasy and nervous manner, yet part of me was relieved at the same time. Jeremy extended the joint, totally secure and maintaining perfect composure, his face conveying that he had fulfilled a long awaited wish.

Everything rested on my taking it from his hand. I knew that this was a defining point in our relationship, perhaps in our lives. Up until this point we had been brothers, close, but not necessarily friends; brothers who still hid things from each other, brothers who still had a wall between them because of age mostly, but also because I held a feeling of responsibility, a sense of duty that mother had engrained in me throughout childhood. I hesitated. Things would change between us. I wanted badly for us to be friends, to be closer, but something in the back of my mind told me it would be a mistake.

In a sudden flash I remembered the years of father staying drunk and mother who I now rarely saw because she was in a Texas jail for credit card fraud, the result of her worsening drug problem. How terrifying that I might become like them but even more so for my brother! These thoughts raced through my mind in the few seconds that I stared at the joint.

Then I gave in. I grabbed it, not looking once into my brother's eyes, shameful almost, as if I knew a bad omen would befall me, and I took a puff.

"Man, I'm happy I'm here for this family moment. This is so special," Bubba said sarcastically with his hand rested on my shoulder.

I feigned a half smile and looked at my brother standing more cheerful than ever. This moment meant the world to him. I tried my best to act cool, to maintain my composure like the rest of them. In all honesty, the reprieve from being so secretive lifted a weight from my shoulders. Mother always said truth prevails. Hell, I was old enough to smoke. But was my brother?

The remainder of the trip passed like an intoxicated dream, allowing the pent up anxiety in my body to expel itself in an unwholesome manner. Lingering until an undetermined time in the future were the consequences of my actions. Until then, we smoked the weekend away. My brother had his own bag of pot and admitted that he and Bubba had smoked before, a few times in fact. Neither surprised nor angry, I knew it was the first of many secrets we would share. But in the back of my mind something told me that our fate had been altered forever.

VII

School was never his specialty. From the beginning of elementary, teachers and principals alike knew the name 'Jeremy Savage' as a child to reckon with, to watch closely and to keep on a tight leash. At home, the telephone rang frequently with calls complaining about some dramatic incident he had formulated or disaster he had created. The threats to expel him never ceased.

Not that any of these inevitable catastrophes were his fault. Somewhere along the line, in the gradual passing monotony of everyday life, blanketed by reassuring words and dismissed notions, Jeremy had received the short end of the stick. The problem stemmed from a lack of discipline and the proper child rearing essential to becoming a healthy, responsible, mature adult. Owning an already fervent colossal amount of unmanaged pent up energy, he had no idea how to regulate or control it. Fate never gave him a chance.

The year after I graduated Jeremy entered ninth grade with his energy full throttle. Full of school spirit, he soon became the school mascot, a Horn Lake Eagle, with every intention of being the greatest mascot the school had ever witnessed. Except the role did not last as long as planned. Constantly skipping school, disrupting class, and rarely doing assignments, Jeremy stayed in detention or suspended. Instead of steering him in the right direction, the principal seemed to do everything in his power to make Jeremy quit.

"It's always that two or three percent causing trouble. We cannot allow them to ruin it for everybody else," the principle often reminded the students over the intercom and at school assemblies. He stood only a few inches over five feet, a perfect target for ridicule, with a handle bar mustache that resembled the Super Mario Brothers. Students subsequently nicknamed him 'Mario' after the first Nintendo came out.

The so-called small percentage of worthless and intractable students apparently made the school's numbers look bad to the public. Instead of attempting to help those often misguided and struggling teenagers, the principle preferred to systematically weed them out, surreptitiously giving them hell until they dropped out, or did something bad enough to be expelled.

The battle against my brother was over before it

began. Barely into the first semester, after just enough pressure to make him feel 'picked on' by the administration, Jeremy figured that changing schools might solve his problems. He had already spent more time in ALC, an all day detention, than in the classroom. Serving his last day of ALC for his latest transgression, he sat quietly, probably wasting time, but not necessarily misbehaving. He began chewing on a pen top.

"You know better than to chew gum in here. That's another day of ALC young man." The woman who oversaw the detention was probably the oldest teacher in the school, senile with one foot in the grave.

"I'm not chewing gum. It's a pen top." Already the anger on Jeremy's face became visible.

"I don't like to be talked back to and I 'specially don't like being lied to. Make it another week."

"Look. I got it here in my hand." He held up the pen top to show her. She ignored him and would not even look his way.

"Look right here!" Jeremy rose from the seat, his short temper ready to explode.

"Sit down or I will call Mr. Bartlett." She stared into his eyes right past the chewed up pen top he held in his hands. Even if she had made a mistake, her pride prohibited her from changing her mind.

"Fuck this shit!" Jeremy knocked a pile of books from her desk, walked out of the classroom and left Horn Lake forever.

Too young to quit, when it came time to transfer, Jeremy needed paperwork filled out and a favorable reference from Horn Lake. Until he returned the eagle outfit, the school refused to do anything. Not that Jeremy needed or even wore the costume, but he thought it was cool to keep. The mask had since been converted into a type of pipe to smoke marijuana, the apparent closed-in space providing a better high as a person was trapped in an engulfing cloud of smoke.

After realizing he would never get into another school without returning the costume, he reluctantly returned it, the pot smell permanently ingrained to forever remember him by. Days later, he entered Overton, a large public school in Memphis. To his surprise, the first day he walked outside and saw students smoking cigarettes.

"It's OK to smoke here?" he asked, trying to make new friends and conversation.

"Sure. The teachers hardly ever come outside."

"Cool. Can I bum a cigarette then?"

"Sure."

After lighting the cigarette, the others walked inside. Jeremy stood there for a few more minutes and then an adult walked out, the dean of discipline.

"What do you think you're doing out here?"

Realizing the pointlessness of lying, Jeremy answered, "Smoking."

"Well, we don't tolerate that type of behavior at this school. Leave the property and do not return." His words were clear and concrete.

"What? It's only my first day. I didn't mean to…"

"You heard me. Don't make me call the law."

Jeremy left the campus cursing the dean with a depressed feeling that he interpreted as anger. He called for a ride home determined to begin school somewhere else the next day.

And he did. Kirby High School was near mom's house. Though conveniently close, after a few short weeks, Jeremy was ready to transfer yet again. As with every other school, he never gave Kirby a chance, missing more days than attending, always creating excuses to leave. Nothing was wrong with the school. He made new friends quickly and easily, possessing a natural charm and a personality envied by even those who disliked him. Still, he decided Kirby was not the place for him.

At the beginning of what should have been his tenth grade year, he tried one more school closer to father's house in Mississippi. Like schools, he switched parents just as often, depending on who catered to him at the moment. Divorces often allow a child to choose between parents, the mother and father wanting nothing more than to please the child, or, perhaps as an act of animosity towards the estranged ex-spouse.

The final attempt at school was pointless. Whatever thoughts raced through his chaotic mind, Jeremy never went enough to accomplish anything worthwhile. On the first request, my father had no problem with him dropping out, failed to even argue against it. He figured Jeremy would get his GED and move on; life would be hunky dory, swell, peaches and cream. Everything would eventually work out great. Dad failed to see the consequences of being a friend instead of a father.

VIII

Almost simultaneously and against natural circumstances, both Jeremy and I entered the adult world, the world of money and bills and responsibility, the world parents warn kids about throughout our childhood but we refuse to prepare for and accept, assuming with some instilled false sense of hope that money will automatically fall into our laps or we will get rich the moment we turn into adults. No rational reason justifies such naivety. No clear idea exists of how money will appear, only that it will be there waiting and life will be just fine. We idealistically believe we might be famous or important in some way, perhaps an entrepreneur, perhaps something to do with computers, television or movies. Life is still young with limitless possibilities.

Then reality hits, cold and relentless, no shame or mercy. Most people end up in the monotony of a regular job with regular pay, working where we never saw ourselves. Life laughs after anxiously waiting all those years, like it warned us, like it was meant to be this way. Live with it.

Though I worked during high school and my parents rarely helped me financially, I soon learned that they helped more than I realized. Eighteen came and went, and still I lived at home. My worthless rants and empty promises about moving out faded to the back of my mind the moment I became an adult. My parents didn't care if I stayed under their roof after I turned eighteen, or maybe they did, but they never threatened to kick me out as long as I did something constructive with my life.

College remained the only option. Not yet sure about the future, I knew I didn't want to end up living the life of my parents. So many times they expressed their regrets about returning to the south from California, about not finishing college, and about marrying each other.

"You two are the only good that ever came out of our marriage," they both often expressed wholeheartedly.

The fall after high school graduation I registered at the local two-year community college. After barely squeaking past high school, a real university would have slapped me in the face. Unaware of the nature of studying, I quickly realized that I needed to put forth an effort. Even at the community college I struggled, but realized that without an education, I would live a life of mediocrity working a forty-hour workweek in a profession I didn't want. Or worse, I would end up at the bottom of the barrel, maybe with an addiction problem like my parents, struggling to get high or just to get by. Already, friends my age were heading in that direction.

Less ready for the real world was Jeremy. Only sixteen, farther from an adult in mind than in age, he had no choice but to get a job. Without a high school diploma, college was not an option. Even his GED was temporarily put off so he could earn money. He found a job at a pizza place as a cook.

Determined to do well and still owning the impenetrable idealism of the young, Jeremy worked full time, asking off only to practice with his new band. His heart and soul lived and breathed for music. Beginning almost out of the womb with a set of drums and working his way up to the piano, the bass and the guitar, he took after my father as a natural musician. He possessed the ability to play almost any instrument upon contact. With an unassailable confidence, he vainly practiced in front of the mirror, put on concerts for the family, and made cassette tapes of himself. In his mind he felt destined to become a star.

Childhood also showed the first signs of his addictive personality. Instead of simply liking a particular band, Jeremy worshipped them. For significant periods of time, no other music existed except what he liked, to the point where anybody else that spent time with him was sick and tired of the same shit over and over again. He bought magazines, covered the walls in his room with posters, and even attempted to dress like the members of the band.

His first obsession was the country band Alabama, especially after we saw them in concert.

"Why country? Why do you have to listen to country?" I could never understand his reasoning.

"I like it." Not a sound explanation in my opinion.

Then he listened to Stryper, a religious rock band who I liked as well so didn't tire of as quickly, and who we also saw in concert.

"Momma, I want to meet them, can we meet them?" Jeremy grabbed my mother's hand and pulled her toward the stage at Mud Island after the show. He figured since we met Alabama, it would be just as easy to meet any other band.

"Sorry, this area is restricted. You have to know someone in the band." A skinny rent-a-cop stood at the entrance to a narrow hall that led backstage.

"Momma, I want to meet them!" Tears began to roll down his face. Mom and dad didn't know how to react.

"It's OK baby, we can't meet them all. Maybe next time." She gave one of those '*I can't believe you said no to this poor child*' looks to the security guard.

A roadie who witnessed the scene must have had a soft heart. He rested his hand on Jeremy's head and said,

"You really want to meet Stryper, don't you? You must like them a whole lot."

"Uh huh." He grinned.

The roadie escorted us backstage where we met and took pictures with the band. Afterwards, we were Stryper's biggest fans for quite awhile, putting on shows in our living room together, Jeremy playing the drums and me with the air guitar and lip-synching. I never picked up the actual ability to play well but feigned perfectly. I figured I would do better at the business end.

The next phase was again country music, Garth Brooks, and it dragged on forever. I began watching my brother turn into a redneck and I supposed it was because we had moved to Mississippi with father. Almost everyone around us was a country fan, so I figured Jeremy, easily influenced, would remain one as well.

"Turn that shit off!" I yelled at him and his friends when they locked his bedroom door and blasted the music while my parents were gone. He probably did it in spite of me because as soon as I yelled he turned it up louder. Thank god he eventually moved on to Aerosmith.

As he grew older and around the time he dropped out of school, his horizons expanded. He made new friends who shared musical interests and they formed a band called Dead Buddha. The guitar player, Mike, had an attitude problem that weighed him down and overshadowed his true talent, but he also was a good bullshitter with connections to the local music scene. This allowed the band to play shows in different clubs around town, even on Beale Street in Memphis. Before long, they collected a cult-like following of teenagers around the area. Jeremy was living his dream at a young age.

Fully supportive of my brother, I went to as many

shows as possible. I loved to witness the raw energy, the passion of the young souls playing their own music on stage. I loved the crowds looking up to and respecting Jeremy. More than anything, I wanted us both to live out our dreams and be successful. He had seemingly found his.

Around the same time our paths began to take different directions in life, as if my strength complemented his weakness and vice versa. It seemed when I was doing well, he was getting into trouble, but when I had problems, his life stayed on track, as if some unknown force larger than ourselves had given us a certain amount of luck to share and we had to figure out how to balance it. Yet we remained closer than ever before and shared everything imaginable. Of course I was still more hesitant about letting him borrow my things than he was with me, but he grew more mature, at least making an effort to take care of my possessions. We took road trips to every concert possible, hung out at the same places, had many of the same friends, and even had sex with the same girls. Nothing could separate us.

As young adults, we were almost free from our parents' grip, from their stifling burden that had held us down for so long. We were at the impervious age where their influence on our psyches might be noticed by others, but not ourselves. Our idealistic visions of the future had not yet been tested, our personalities not fully realized. The young individual moves forward in a state of constant transition, but to him the future and the past are insignificant. Only the present matters. The past is over and the future will take care of itself, still so far away and full of artificial hope.

IX

Two years of junior college, an absolute necessity after my grades in high school and if I wanted to enter a real university, paved the way to my becoming a Tennessee Volunteer in Knoxville. August would soon arrive, and I expected to pack my bags and leave Mississippi on my own for the first time in my life. Naturally I was excited, but part of me would miss home, my friends, and especially my brother. I wondered how he would fare without me around.

For years we had planned to take a road trip to the West coast, California our prime destination. Jeremy had dreamed of going to the Golden state his entire life. The stars lived there, and with the never-ending ambition to be famous, he swore he would live there as well. Realizing I would be gone for at least a year or two, the time was ripe to make the trip.

From the beginning it seemed to be doomed. We had little money, but that problem was soon solved when grandma gave us her gas card to fill up along the way. Then, the night before we left, Jeremy and his guitar player were arrested for selling weed on Beale

Street after a show they played. I had almost given up on the trip, but later the same evening, after father bailed him out of jail, Jeremy walked in the door smiling,

"You ready or what?"

"Are you serious? You still want to go?"

"Hell yeah. We been planning this forever."

I turned and stared at father in disbelief. For a second, I thought he would say something.

"You're still letting him go?" I asked when he said nothing.

"It's probably good for him to get out of here for a while."

The last thing I wanted was to cancel the Western tour, but I thought for sure father would put his foot down. Once again, he sat passively by and played friend rather than father.

"OK then. Pack up and let's go."

"Already have." Jeremy walked to his room and appeared seconds later with a duffle bag, a small suitcase, and his guitar. "But hey, mind if I get a shower first? Jail stinks."

Nothing like the open road. Pure freedom. The windows down and the breeze blowing as we drove shirtless, the sun beating through the glass and unevenly tanning the side of our body hanging out of the window. No real destination, no time constraints. Sure, I had to be back in August for school, but if we found a place we liked enough, maybe we would stay for good. School could wait.

The first stop was our other grandmother's house in Hot Springs, Arkansas to get extra money. Our parents didn't give us a dime, but we could always rely on our grandparents. Their generation was dependable, the ones who worked and saved and had been through a World War. They knew the value of a dollar. For some reason my parents' generation had screwed everything up, former hippies, getting life spoon fed to them and never learning responsibility. Most of them were dysfunctional and dependent upon their parents.

"How will my parents manage when my grandparents aren't around any more?" I often wondered.

"Man, Oklahoma sure is dull." Jeremy stretched out in the passenger seat staring out of the window. It appeared desolate and lifeless, flat, green, the Sooner state, whatever that meant. Some guys our age confirmed our suspicions when they said they used to live in West Memphis, Arkansas, and it was more fun than Oklahoma.

To pass our time we played trivia with state capitals and nicknames.

"Capital of Rhode Island?"

"Providence." Jeremy was surprisingly sharp for someone without a high school diploma.

Kansas was almost as bad, but at least we could play guessing games about the endless crops growing, doing our best trying to figure out if we were looking at wheat, barley, or something else.

"Is that Hard Red Winter wheat or white wheat?"

"How the hell should I know? Where did you hear those terms?"

"Saw 'em on a sign earlier. I wonder where they filmed Superman, if it was really in Kansas."

"Looks like it."

We hoped to see a tornado but had no luck. Worse, it was Sunday and every radio station played church sermons or Christian music. We turned off the radio, sang 80's songs to ourselves for a while, and sped to get out of the state as fast as possible.

After the Midwest, the country became more interesting. We drove through Colorado, stopping at Denver and then Boulder. Then we made our way through Wyoming, without a doubt the most beautiful state in the country and with the least amount of people. There were plenty of spots to camp for free in the parks, and if they weren't free, we just packed up and left early in the morning before a ranger spotted us. Every time we told ourselves the sites couldn't get better, we were surprised again on what the country had to offer. We had been trapped in the south for too long.

Youth also had advantages. Countless kids our age were doing the same as us, taking extended road trips. While we eventually planned to return home, others drifted from city to city, finding new jobs here and there, permanently on the road like Jack Kerouac, searching for something besides the monotony of everyday life. Many offered us places to stay, bud to smoke, and told us about sites to visit, festivals to attend, and where to find the best drugs. There was no shortage of information to guide our way.

Passing through the rolling green hills and ranches of Montana finally led us to Spokane, Washington, where a friend of ours, JB, was staying. He had moved the previous year from Mississippi, mainly to get his life on track. Like so many others we knew and counting, he allowed the tedium of the south to bring him down and began getting into trouble. In Spokane, he was about to get his GED and had a well-paying job.

JB's home offered us the first real beds of the trip and proved comfortable and refreshing. He introduced us to many new faces, including one beautiful girl who I wanted to take home. Straight black hair and natural in the modern-day hippie sense of the word, Moriah was beautiful. She knew all the areas around town to see the best views. Our few days spent in Spokane together, we sat atop mountains and cliffs watching the sunset and then the stars. We smoked the best pot we had ever smoked and talked about life. Though I wanted to stay longer, JB had decided to return to Memphis after his GED graduation. Jeremy and I moved on.

In nearby Seattle we walked the streets and visited the major attractions but were super-anxious to get to California. Only first, I wanted to stop at the Rainbow Gathering. From Colorado to Washington, at almost every stop someone had mentioned the gathering, making it sound like a utopian fantasy that all individuals should experience.

"Man, your trip won't be complete without going to the Rainbow Gathering. It will change your life forever."

"You'll never want to leave. It's the way the world should be."

Jeremy wasn't as anxious but acquiesced, at least to check it out.

After driving miles into the heart of the Oregon forest thinking we were lost, cars with environmentally friendly bumper stickers and Volkswagen vans assured that we were traveling in the right direction. We followed the vehicles and the temporary makeshift signs hanging from the trees but not nailed, as nailing them would be disrespectful and damaging to Mother Earth. Eventually we came upon a huge parking lot where a man with dreadlocks and dingy homemade clothing haphazardly directed traffic.

"Welcome home brothers." Another guy who hadn't taken a bath in weeks came up and hugged us not long after we got out of the car. He pointed in the direction of a trail.

Along the trail to the campsites others did the same, not all hugging, but everyone smiling and chanting the same words,

"Welcome home brothers."

Jeremy and I looked at each other, both amazed at this newly discovered world within the forest. The unimpeded beating of bongo drums further guided us down the right path. Small campsites were set up, some with only a few people, others with several families, babies and pets, children walking around barefoot, some butt naked. Many people looked as if they had lived there for weeks or even months.

Luckily, we brought along a tent. With plenty of open space, we found a secluded spot, not too far from the main campfire where the bongos beat non-stop, but far enough to have a little peace and tranquility. In my mind, I had found a temporary home. The thought of living communally with a total absence of technology and in the wilderness captivated me.

After only a few days, Jeremy missed his McDonald's cheeseburgers and the air conditioning of the car. He had seen enough and wanted to leave.

"C'mon man. This is an awesome experience." I tried to persuade him to stay longer. "Have you ever seen people live this way?"

Everyone shared food, drugs, and every other item on their person. At night, the campfire became a huge bonfire where dancing, instruments and chanting gave way to an unparalleled energy found only in individuals who were able to let go of the inhibitions and civilities of the modern world. Joints and pot brownies were ceaselessly distributed, everybody, including Jeremy and I contributing our fair share.

"Yeah, it's cool. I'm ready for some real food though. Plus, I could use a bath." We ate rice, beans, and the few snacks we had left over. No money was accepted. Only the barter system was used. At first, we had a difficult time buying anything. Then we began trading things like our pot, older T-shirts and extra blankets. In return, we were given food, drugs, and other worthless but cool trinkets to take home.

Eventually I gave in. Not really because he kept complaining, but because the nights were cold, almost unbearable with our lack of clothing, and I was beginning to crave real food as badly as Jeremy. We were used to the humid summer months of the south, not Oregon's cold nights. The last thing I wanted to do was sleep near the fire in the dirt and mud like some of the people there did. Maybe I was too civilized or dependent on modern day comforts, but I could handle only so much of the communal lifestyle. We left for California.

By now, the car was filthy and stinking. Most of our clothes were dirty and we had not taken a bath in a few days. Only the strong smell of sage given to us by a hippie couple who rode with us after the Gathering overpowered the stench. Three weeks together and every little idiosyncrasy began to get on each other's nerves. I especially got angry when Jeremy continued to pick his nose and wipe it on the steering wheel.

"That's fuckin' nasty man. Quit doin' that shit. I gotta drive too."

"What are you talkin' about?" He acted innocent and unaware.

"You know what I'm talkin' about, pickin' your fuckin' nose and then wipin' it on the steering wheel."

"Am not."

I waited patiently for him to do it again. When he had his finger in his nose, I hit the bottom of his hand hard, making his finger dig deeper. His big brown eyes watered with pain.

"Mother fucker! That hurt!" The car veered to the side of the road.

"Watch where you're going."

"Don't do that shit again, man. I'm not kidding."

"Quit pickin' your nose and wiping it on my steering wheel."

"I won't. Just don't do that again or we'll be

fighting."

"Whatever."

"Whatever."

It was the closest we came to a fight on the entire trip. After spending twenty-four seven with someone for so long, even the smallest things can annoy. Nevertheless, we laughed it off later. I could think of no one else who I would rather have been traveling with.

In California, we had another place to reenergize our bodies for a few days. David, a friend of Jeremy's, lived with his mother and her roommates in Santa Rosa. Like JB, David attempted to escape the problems of Mississippi by moving to the other side of the country. Also like JB, he was doing well, holding a steady job and staying out of trouble. Sometimes all it took was a change of scenery.

David first took us to Bodega Bay, where we climbed gigantic rocks in the ocean and searched for starfish. Then, we traveled to San Francisco three days in a row, a chaotic city, but full of vibrant and eclectic life. We walked through China Town, where dead animals hung in windows ready to be cooked and the language was uninterpretable. We visited Haight and Ashbury, where there were more homeless and headshops than I had ever seen.

"Bud. Hashish. LSD." People walked freely down the street offering drugs, especially pot. At night we returned to Santa Rosa, not far, and drank and smoked until we passed out. So far California had been an intoxicated dream full of new faces, crowds of people and exotic happenings, so different from home. It was difficult to take it all in at once.

Not only had we maxed out grandma's gas card buying gas and food, but we were almost broke. We would be lucky to get home, much less visit L.A., the place we, or at least Jeremy, wanted to visit most. We called grandma.

"Well, we can probably get home with what we have, but we still want to visit Hollywood, and maybe the Grand Canyon on the way home."

"Aren't you going to Disneyland?"

"Grandma, we can't afford that. We were just wondering if you could send us a little bit to get home on."

"Well, I'll tell you what. I'll send a few hundred dollars, but promise me you'll go to Disneyland. You know, we took you there when you were only six months old. And your brother, he's been to

Disneyworld, but not Disneyland."

"I promise. Thanks so much, grandma."

"You two just make it home safe. We miss ya. You'll be able to talk about this road trip for the rest of your life."

"That's for sure."

We headed for Disneyland immediately after we picked up our money from Western Union. We smoked a huge joint before entering the park and then rode Space Mountain three times and everything else we could before the park closed. That night we stayed in a nice hotel with a swimming pool.

"Thank God for grandmas," Jeremy remarked after a hot shower.

Finally we arrived to Los Angeles. Jeremy's eyes stayed wide open searching for somebody famous. We walked through Beverly Hills, down the Sunset Strip and into the Whiskey-A-Go-Go where a heavy metal Japanese band played on stage. We didn't understand a word but they rocked. Jeremy went into every record company we came across and tried to find somebody to give his Dead Buddha demo tapes. Some took them, others declined.

Again we were next to broke. We searched the

beach, hoping to find a place to sleep. Cops patrolled nearby, so we found a parking lot and slept in the car. In the early morning, a tap on the windshield awoke us.

"Guys, wake up." A cop not much older than me had his face to the glass. The early morning sun blinded me. "You know it's illegal to sleep here?"

"Really?" I played dumb although we had read the sign earlier. "The truth is we're about broke and wanted to save our last bit of money to go to Disneyland. You wouldn't happen to know the quickest way from here would you?" It was a weak attempt at changing the subject but worked.

"Sure. Where you guys from?"

"Mississippi." Jeremy and I said it in unison. The cop gave us detailed directions and allowed us to leave without any questions or citations, a nice cop, again an unexpected surprise.

"Too bad we already been to Disneyland. Sucker." We laughed and headed to the final destination of our road trip.

The Grand Canyon appeared bottomless except for the tiny groove of the blue river that ran through it.

"Man, it's so awesome here. There's so many beautiful places in the world, just in the United States even. And we get stuck in fuckin' Mississippi. Why the hell did mom and dad ever move from California?" Jeremy stared out into the canyon. We found a perfect rock to sit on, peaceful, and at the time away from the tourists.

"I don't know. I guess because that's where their family is. I've asked them the same question plenty of times. I think they regret it, but hey, I guess it's too late now."

"Not for us. We're still young, man. We can move anywhere we want. In a couple of years or less, I'm movin' to California. Los Angeles. I'll be a musician or an actor one. Did you see all the shit goin' on? This trip makes me realize how much there is out there. It gives me motivation. And when ya think about it, California's really not so far away."

"True."

"You're gonna move with me right?" He looked at me intently as if it was the most serious question he had ever posed.

"Hell ya. I've been wantin' to get out of Memphis as long as I can remember. That's why I'm going to school in Knoxville. Not so far away, but still, away for a while. Away from family, from all the bullshit that's accumulated over the course of our life. Almost like a new start, ya know? I see all my friends, still doing the same thing, gettin' high and drunk all the time, not doing anything with their lives. They'll probably never change."

"Well, we can both have a new beginning in California."

"I hope so."

"You don't sound so positive, bro."

"I just hope everything turns out good for us, you know? We've been through so much shit. Sometimes the future looks rough, like everything is a dream and will always be a dream. You get to a point in life and say, 'Damn. I'm twenty-two already. This isn't where I expected to be.' I mean, don't get me wrong, I'm not saying we can't do it, I'm just saying it's not as easy as just saying it."

"The we gotta DO it. We'll both make it. It's gonna take both of setting our minds to it, but together we can accomplish anything we want. You got the brains and I got the talent."

"I know. What if something happens to one of us though?"

"Don't talk like that. I'd go crazy if something

happened to you. Lose my mind. I'd probably end up jumpin' off into this canyon here." We both looked down. "You know I've always looked up to you. You're the only sane one in the family, the one goin' to school and gettin' an education. Probably have a good job soon and a wife and kids. You know, all the normal stuff in life."

"Maybe. But in California, somewhere besides the south."

"There you go. The both of us."

The stars and moon began to show against the black night. The bottom of the canyon could no longer be seen but it could be felt, as if it bragged about its vast character, its majestic and endless magnitude. Jeremy and I sat staring into the dark void. We attempted to name constellations, the Big and Little Dipper the only ones we really knew for sure. Those years in Boy Scouts had taught me little in that respect.

We smoked the rest of the bud we had bought. It seemed so much better than in the south, like everything else. Though the night was still young, it seemed late, and we wanted to be out of the park before morning to avoid paying camping fees, especially since we were almost out of money. The empty highway led us to a rest area a good ways outside of the park. We stopped and slept in the car until the heat of the morning sun woke us up. Then we headed back home, broke, and without any pot left. We even had to steal gas a few times. After a month on the road, we were determined and motivated to go home and plan for the future, a future outside of Mississippi.

X

Knoxville proved to be the most peaceful period of my life. With nobody I knew living there, it was my first opportunity to be distanced from family, to make new friends, and to contemplate things away from the monotony of Mississippi. The time away from home helped me realize the importance of planning the future. For so long I had lived in the present and disregarded my future, naively expecting everything to just fall in place. Though still young with my life far from predetermined, my world was being shaped and I realized I had to do the shaping in order to get what I wanted.

During those two years, Jeremy visited a few times. Once he stayed over a week in my dorm. Though we still went out and partied, I was intent on doing well in class and keeping up my grades, so I decided to give him some assignments during the school week to keep him busy.

"How about I make you some assignments while you're here, stuff that will help you study? That way you won't get bored during the day while I'm in class and maybe you'll be more ready for the GED when you decide to take it." Not having a high school diploma remained a source of negative self-esteem and I figured he needed a push in the right direction.

"Sure, why not? I need to take it soon anyway, before I forget everything I've learned." At home, he still had his band, still worked the pizza job, but academically had taken no steps towards getting his GED.

Hopefully the time spent doing the schoolwork helped, but I could not control his life at home. Every time I talked to him he explained,

"Oh yeah, yeah. I been workin' on all that stuff you gave me. I'll be able to take the test before too long. I just want to be ready."

He never took the test. Something always 'came up' or he wasn't 'quite ready'. Against my better judgment, I finally left him alone about the issue thinking it might further butcher his self-esteem if I kept nagging. As far as I knew from my ivory tower in Knoxville, he was getting along fine without an education. I learned differently when I returned home.

XI

Like a Boy Scout Jeremy was prepared for our road trip to New Orleans. The amount of drugs he brought could only be guesstimated so I drove the speed limit, incessantly staring into the rear view mirror.

"Man, you done got paranoid in your old age," Jeremy teased sarcastically. "I told ya if we get caught I'll tell 'em it's mine and you didn't know nothin' about it."

For some reason this statement did not ease my mind. After returning from college in Knoxville, I had begun a career as a schoolteacher. My days of drug use had basically come to an end except for smoking pot and maybe an ecstasy pill on special occasions. The annual Voodoo Festival on Halloween qualified as one of those. Every time I traveled to New Orleans something crazy happened.

The city possessed a sinister vibe as though it bred immorality. While visiting, people seemed to let down their inhibitions. The dark side of a person's character found room to breathe and express itself for a short time. The shyness found in reason temporarily disappeared.

Though the more historically significant parts of
the city were popular with tourists, the large antebellum
homes and cemeteries with grandiose tombs of stone, I
knew only the district where the smell was comparable
to a sewer. The alleys and streets were filled with urine
and trash. Homeless men and women littered the streets
and begged for change. Con artists who recognized a
tourist at first glance used every trick in the book to get
money.

"Bet I can tell you where you got your shoes," said
a man in cheap, worn out clothing as he stopped causing
me to run into him.

"OK," I said interested during my first trip to New
Orleans, only seconds after setting foot onto Bourbon
Street.

"If I guess right ya gotta give me five dollars."

"Five? I'll give ya two." I knew he would pull
some trick but wanted to hear his answer.

"You got them on your feet." He smiled with
more than a tooth missing and stuck out his hand. For
the next half hour he followed my friend and I and tried
to be our tour guide, naturally for extra money.

New Orleans symbolized the rest of the country's
waste flowing south and emptying into the Gulf, like a

giant toilet waiting to get flushed. It needed a good cleaning.

"Man, tell me you don't have a lot of stuff. Only enough for us, right?"

"I brought a little extra just so I could pay my way. I don't want you payin' for everything."

A little extra could mean any amount. Jeremy had a profession as the dope-man now, getting ecstasy tablets dirt cheap and killer bud by the pound. I knew exactly where the profit went. He liked to party no doubt; long nights at the strip club where he sold most of his product, road trips to see his favorite bands, alcohol and drugs for himself. In the end he had nothing to show for it all. Sooner or later he would get caught.

The Hilton hotel and casino had a perfect view of the mighty Mississippi flowing into the Gulf, the muddy river racing to get a breath in the sea and purify itself. We knew the hotel would not be cheap but I saved enough for most of the trip and Jeremy promised to pay his half. Possibly we might win some money in the casino. We unpacked our bags and wasted no time getting to Bourbon Street.

The following day was Voodoo Festival. An annual event, this year our favorite band Tool was headlining, the main reason we were there. Tool represented an indescribable significance for us, the off time music for Jeremy and the spiritually profound lyrics for me. The band was our shared obsession. Though we would certainly watch the other bands, we drove to New Orleans with Tool in mind.

No sooner had I showered than I spotted Jeremy counting ecstasy on the polished wooden desk of the hotel room. At least fifty pills were scattered chaotically about the top.

"Damn! There's no way we're taking all those. I thought you said you only had enough for us."

"I did say I had enough for us. I just brought a few extra to get rid of." He gave me a sinister grin.

Nothing could be done now. I shook my head a little pissed but decided to go with the flow.

"Just be careful. Sometimes at these shows undercover cops try to set ya up to bust ya." I always felt it was my duty to offer big brotherly advice.

"Most of these are for people I'm supposed to meet down here. I won't sell to anyone I don't know."

Jeremy could be so full of shit. He made a habit of lying through his teeth and unfortunately believed every word he said. He would sell to anybody that could pay for the pills, especially once he was fucked up himself. Sometimes he got so messed up on his own stuff he became sloppy, losing money and drugs.

On the outskirts of the city in a large area spanning at least a few hundred acres, people were strewn everywhere. As we parked the car my brother pulled out a prescription bottle and took out a couple of yellow tablets.

"These are the strong ones, the best. We'll just take one now and maybe one later right before Tool begins."

"Ok." I stared into his hand excited. I trusted him. With one last gulp from a beer I had gotten from the hotel room I swallowed the pill. Jeremy did the same. We smiled at each other.

"Ready?"

"Hell ya! Let's go."

An eclectic atmosphere filled the air, hundreds of people from every walk of life drinking, smoking, yelling and ready to see their favorite band. Most of them were already high, some just getting started, others well past fucked up. The October sun beat down transforming a naturally cool fall day into a mildly warm one. Capitalists encircled the entire festival with everything from five-dollar bottles of water and eight-dollar beers to hemp necklaces and incense, something for every consumer.

By the time Jeremy and I were inside and within distance of the main stage, the ecstasy had begun to take affect. Slowly, an acute awareness of our surroundings seeped into my being. Every noise, movement, expression and object caught my attention, as if I was able to absorb all the individual components of life at once and form a greater whole. My senses were keener, my mind seemingly interconnected with the larger collective consciousness.

When Jeremy and I looked at each other we smiled, knowing exactly what the other was thinking. Our drug trips before led to hours on end of deep conversations and secrets revealed. Ecstasy and other Hellohallucinogens like it brought subconscious feelings to the surface. Later today we would do the same thing; discuss our hopes and fears, our dreams and desires, impress on each other our different worldviews and ultimately hope we would accomplish all our dreams together in the future.

We explored the different booths where old hippies and African immigrants sold trinkets, talked with many beautiful girls who caught our eye, and socialized with anyone who appeared to be in our same state of mind. Every other person fit this description or wanted to fit it. Jeremy had already begun to sell his product, easily getting $30 a pill. By this time I was completely detached from any immediate ongoing happenings, and conversing with anyone who stopped to talk.

From the corner of his eye Jeremy noticed a table full of sunglasses for sale. A pair with ethereal red lenses especially caught his attention.

"Whoa! We got to get us a pair of these. Check 'em out."

I put the glasses on and immediately felt I had changed realities.

"For real. These make everything so much cooler right now."

Luckily, the African with dreads had two identical pairs and we bought them both. We then made our way towards the main stage and sat on the comfortable lush green grass away from possible cops or security. Jeremy had rolled a few joints to bring along, took one from his cigarette pack and lit it.

"These glasses are fuckin' crazy, ya know it?

Everything is just so much more vivid right now."

"Here. Let me see what your reality looks like. You can see mine." We exchanged glasses.

"Whoa. Your reality is psycho. This is some crazy shit. It's like I can feel everything you go through. Man, we're livin' totally different lives bro."

"Yeah, I feel it too. You think you could handle my reality for a long time?"

"Don't know. Let's trade for the day and see. Maybe I'll be able to understand you a little better or maybe I'll end up losing my mind."

"Cool." Anybody hearing or watching us probably thought we were crazy or perhaps they understood perfectly, at least those who were in a similar state of mind. Ecstasy opened up a window of perception. It made the user believe that he had encountered some surreptitious truth to life, some way to resolve the world's problems.

"Man, ya know if everybody in the world took this drug at one time there would be no more fighting. Israel and Palestine, India and Pakistan, Muslims and Christians, husbands and wives. Who knows what could be accomplished? People need to experience this, at least one good time, just to know how it feels. There has to be a way to keep this feeling, reach a higher consciousness where everybody sees what we see and yet we're still productive in society."

"I love it when you're trippin' bro. You get so philosophical but it makes so much sense. I feel ya. I know what ya mean." Jeremy peered around through his red glasses to make sure no one was looking. "It's about that time. Want another one?"

"Sure." Again he had saved the last two yellow pills for us. We swallowed them with our beer and sat for a while more talking and staring at the large grassy field filling up more rapidly with people now as the bigger name bands began to play.

My last memory was Missy Elliot rapping. I remembered thinking she sounded good. Losing coherence, I seemed to be lucid only at intervals for the remainder of the night. I remembered walking around and trying to engage people in conversation though I doubted they understood me. I never remembered losing my brother or him losing me.

When I regained control of my senses I was somehow in front of the stage and watching Tool. My ears first recognized the slow, melancholy, instrumental guitar part of track eleven on Lateralus. It seemed to carry on and on, more sustained and prolonged than I had ever heard. Every varying pitch caught my attention. Then the song blasted into another, faster paced and heavy, awakening me from some soporific dream state. I had blacked out for most of the night. I studied my surroundings. From my chest to my feet, as if I had been swimming, I was soaking wet, shoes and all. No pool of water was in sight but I slightly remembered a small pond somewhere. I wondered how many bands I had missed and where my brother had gone.

Sooner or later we would find each other so I watched the rest of the concert. It lasted only a few songs more. The end of the concert meant the end of Voodoo Festival so I headed towards the car in search of Jeremy. I felt in my pocket and my head for the conscious altering red sunglasses. They were nowhere to be found. Crushed, I felt as if I had thrown away a precious destiny, a redeemable reality.

Jeremy found me first. He was talking with some friends from Memphis.

"Damn, what happened to you? Why you all wet?"

"Honestly I have no idea. I lost it there for a

while. Don't remember much."

Everyone laughed and continued talking about the different bands. Jeremy and I soon returned to the hotel. Still wide-awake and barely tripping, we were ready to return to Bourbon Street. After a long hot shower and a change of clothes, the rest of the night was spent getting rid of excess ecstasy and allowing our demons to continue exposing themselves in the city of wickedness.

XII

The way my brother avoided me seemed eerie and unnatural. After our trip to New Orleans, I devoted myself to work, not expecting another break for a while. Between finishing college and my job, I had little time for family or friends. Still, days passed when I tried to call or stop by Jeremy's apartment, possibly to hang out or just to see how he was doing. He lived within walking distance yet I rarely saw him.

New Year's Eve arrived and my roommate and I threw a huge party in our apartment. We bought three kegs of cheap beer, the kind that caused a headache the next morning, with the expectation our place would be packed. Jeremy showed up with ecstasy to sell to anyone wanting to bring in the New Year in an alternative state of mind.

After midnight I noticed him talking to several shady looking figures that were unfamiliar. They were Hispanic. Not the poor, stereotypical type who looked like they worked construction or got their hands dirty, but they were well dressed and wore excessive gold bracelets and chains. Plenty of people came to the party that I did not recognize but these guys blatantly stood out.

"Who are those guys?" I asked suspiciously when my brother and I were alone.

"They're the ones who supplied the X for tonight. I ran out and needed more so I called them up. It's OK if they're here, right?"

"Sure, sure. I didn't care who was at the party as long as everybody was having fun. "You known them for a long time?"

"For a while, yeah."

"I thought Johnny sold you X?"

"He does, he does. But these guys got it too. Sometimes it's even cheaper."

"OK." The story sounded odd, but at the time I was too drunk to absorb it. "Well, I'm just glad you're here bro. Seems like I don't see you much anymore."

"Yeah, I know. I been working a lot. We'll hang out more though. Matter of fact, let's make it one of our New Year's resolutions." He rested his hand on my shoulder.

"Definitely." I smiled and hoped he was sincere.

While refilling my beer at the almost empty third keg, I watched Jeremy and his new friends. They spoke low and unintelligible, as if they were making some sort of secret business transaction. No doubt they were trying to keep their words quiet. Minutes later, Jeremy walked up and said,

"Hey bro, we're about to head out."

"Already? Man, it's still early. There are plenty of females and alcohol left. Why you gotta go?"

"Things to do, people to see." Then he gave the conniving grin, the one where he knew that you knew he was lying, but he still lied anyway.

"Well, be careful. Happy New Year." I wasn't angry. In fact, I was more worried about getting the beautiful black-headed girl I had been talking to all night into my bedroom. My brother was an adult. I could not monitor his every movement.

Jeremy was now a young man, working, paying rent, and living the life of a bachelor. He didn't need an older brother to tell him how to live. Maybe he grew tired of my lecturing, my constant advice. Or maybe he saw how my life had taken a U-turn. One minute we partied non-stop together and the next I was a somewhat respectable schoolteacher. It was time to grow up and become responsible, or else our dreams of the future would never become reality.

Perhaps Jeremy saw things differently. Maybe he thought I was abandoning our dreams. Maybe the way I had changed had threatened our goals in his mind. The further I advanced, the further he regressed. At first, it wasn't obvious or else I wasn't paying attention. He had always been the one to get into trouble, to act crazy. Part of me wanted to believe he would grow up, that this self-destructive phase of life would pass. The other part, the more rational side, somehow knew he would end up in bad shape. What more could we expect from growing up with parents like ours?

The New Year set in, and again we rarely saw each other. The resolution faded away, but not because of me. I made the extra effort, went out of my way in fact, to stop by his apartment at least every other day. He was rarely there or at least rarely answered the door. When he was there, he still seemed gone, spaced out.

"Man, tell me the truth about something." I finally came to the point where I had to confront him. I sat down on the loveseat in his littered apartment. So many times I had failed to say anything, scared my words would push him further away. I had made references about his drug use in the past, but of course he denied it. He always denied it. Then, finally, I flat out asked him,

"Tell me what's going on, Jeremy. I know you're using something, something more than X or pot, or even alcohol. You're changing man, heading down a dead end road. I can see it. The family can see it. You don't come around much anymore, you don't call. Either you work or stay out all night at the strip clubs selling X. But you ain't got shit to show for it. Nothing. You're apartment is a wreck, you look like shit, you..." I became quiet. I felt I had already overdone it. I looked at Jeremy who still said nothing.

"C'mon bro. It's me you're talking to. I want to help you out if I can."

He sat on the couch and stared at the ground. For a second I thought he was about to cry and then instead of tears, painful words flowed from his mouth.

"I been doin' heroin man. Fuckin' tar. Not for very long, but it's like I can't stop now. Honestly, I love the shit. I love the feeling, but I know it's starting to catch up with me. I been wanting to tell you but I couldn't, I just couldn't." He never took his eyes from the floor.

"I was at the strip club the other night and was fucked up. I brought these two chicks home with me and fucked the shit out of one of them. Next thing I know it's the afternoon, I wake up, and all my pills, all my cash, it's gone. And guess what? So are the females. It's hurtin' my business."

I sat in disbelief. *"Heroin, fucking heroin. No fucking way,"* I thought. And the worse part, Jeremy made no mention of wanting to stop, wanting to clean up. He thought it was bad only because he was losing money.

"I owe Johnny so much fuckin' money, you wouldn't believe. I could have bought a nice ride by now, paid for part of a house even. But what do I do? I blow it. Get fucked up and lose half my shit."

"Damn bro. I had no idea you were into things this deep. I mean, I knew something was wrong, but heroin? When did you start that shit?"

"With the band. We were practicing one night and Thomas had some. Apparently he had been doing it for a while. He asked if we wanted to try it and Mike and I said 'Sure, why not?' And of course Bub, he never even smokes bud, so he didn't want any. He's the smart one of the group."

"Sounds like it. I can't believe it. What now? You can't keep doin' that shit. You have to stop before you get worse." I talked as if I knew he could just stop instantaneously.

"I am, I am. I been planning on quitting for awhile. I guess now's as good as time as any, before I lose my job."

"Or your life. Damn. This is serious, bro. Why don't you try rehab or something?"

"I can get off the stuff. I'm strong-minded, like you. If that don't work, then maybe I'll go, but I want to try myself first."

"Please try. Whatever I can do to help, I will. Just let me know."

"Thanks bro. It's actually a weight off my shoulders telling you. I hate keeping things from you. I been ashamed I guess. That's why I don't come and see you much."

"Don't be ashamed. Just get straight. Please just get straight. This is your life we're talking about. You know how bad our parents are screwed up because of drugs. Don't let the same thing happen to you."

"I'm not."

I stayed late into the night, watching TV. Suddenly, my perception of Jeremy had changed. I was scared to leave him alone. For the past year or two, I had been living vicariously through him. I wanted to be the one playing music all the time, bringing beautiful girls home from the strip club, and making a fortune selling X rather than being responsible and selling out to the real world. Except now the real world of my brother was exposed. He was hurting, trapped, a slave to heroin and I didn't have any idea what to do about it.

I stared at my brother on the couch while he slept and I began to cry. Finally, I got up and left. For the next few months he continued to avoid me. More than ever, my advice became pointless and a threat to his way of living. He just wanted to be left alone.

XIII

Early April brought warm weather with a still tolerable humidity. On a Friday night dampness permeated the air. Incoming rain clouds drowned out the stars in the black night sky and transformed it into a deep purple. With the first indication of temperate weather the downtown streets of Memphis teemed with people, baseball season had opened and Memphis in May was right around the corner. Diverse crowds of residents and tourists lined the streets, cruised in their vehicles and filled the clubs and restaurants. Spring had arrived.

My new girlfriend and I parked as close to the restaurant as possible, hoping the impending rain would wait until our bellies were full and appetites quenched. We walked slowly along the sidewalks because she wore black high heels, probably uncomfortable but amplifying her already beautiful legs. Cars honked as we made our way down Front Street. Though my jealousy had faded with age, I wanted to curse them all but couldn't blame them. She was the epitome of woman.

A young hostess sat us at a table immediately. Within minutes my girl and I were feeling the effects of red wine and staring into each other's eyes, love in its infancy. We shared new conversation, opening up and learning those first idiosyncrasies of one another, careful not to reveal everything for fear of rejection but still bordering on the threshold of deepness. Our thoughts and actions were suspended in time, both impervious to any outside event that might be taking place.

Then my cell phone rang. I ignored it. It rang again. Recognizing the number of my grandmother, I decided to call her back later. Not a minute after it stopped ringing, it rang a third time. Our moment had been spoiled. Thinking it might be a possible emergency I finally answered.

"Hello." I sounded irritated.

"Josh. Where are you?" My grandmother's voice sounded stressed.

"Trying to enjoy dinner out with Niki. What's going on?"

"Oh, I'm sorry." She paused as if she was waiting for me to say it was OK. When I said nothing, she finally spoke. "It's your brother. He's down here in Coldwater. He wants you to come down."

"I'm eating in downtown Memphis. Niki and I have plans tonight. I can't come all the way down there. What's goin' on anyway?" My short temper began to flare as I raised my voice.

"Oh, OK. Well, I'll tell him. I just feel so sorry for him right now."

"What's wrong grandma?" Here came her trademark guilt trip.

"He's sick Josh. Really sick. I think he's going through withdrawals. He's in the back bedroom throwing up and yelling and crying and I feel so bad for him I've never seen him like this I don't know what's wrong he just keeps asking to see his brother. Your dad is back there with him right now. Please come if you can."

"Jesus. I'm in the middle of dinner. Let me call you back." I hung up the phone and looked at Niki wondering if I should tell her the truth or make up a good lie. If she knew about my familial problems this early in the relationship, she would be sure to end it.

"My brother. He's at my grandmother's. He's going through withdrawals." The words came out slowly but clearly as I stared down at the table avoiding contact with her big brown eyes.

"Withdrawals? From what?"

"I think heroin." I paused and tried to make out the expression on her face, then lowered my head. "He admitted to me not too long ago that he had done it a few times. I guess he's done it more than I thought. He wants me to come down and stay with him. I don't know what good it will do. He probably won't even realize I'm there."

"You should go." She lifted my head up gently, resting her small hand on my chin. "It sounds like he's trying to get off of that stuff. He needs you."

"Maybe. He's always been wild, started doing drugs at a young age. I never thought he would get this bad though. He's been acting different lately, avoiding me. I guess now I know why." My mood drastically shifted as I put the pieces of the recent past together in my head.

"Why don't we go ahead and go. We can go out again another time." This beautiful girl across the table seemed so understanding.

"Let's finish dinner first. We've already ordered." I took her hand and looked at her again. Her face showed genuine concern. "And let's take our time. He'll be there all night."

I grabbed my glass of wine and finished it, trying to smile and make conversation but the mood had shifted. We began talking about the history of drugs in my family. I figured I might as well tell her everything at once and drop the bomb. The look on her face told me she felt my pain. I knew I truly loved her at that moment.

I reached Coldwater a few hours later to find my grandmother and father still awake watching TV. My father explained the situation. He had known for some time about Jeremy's drug problem. Like so many times before he fostered an empty idea of hope, that everything would just take care of itself; Jeremy would be fine. What had finally made my brother decide to get clean neither my father nor grandmother could say.

In the back room Jeremy lay on the bed motionless but with eyes wide open staring at nothing, a Tool CD playing on the stereo and a bucket filled with vomit next to the bed. A dim nightlight illuminated a weary unshaven face, oblivious to the world.

"Bro. You alright?"

Like a dead body awakened, Jeremy raised his head and stared at me with empty eyes.

"Josh?" His voice struggled. He looked straight at me like a blind man calling out because he could hear my voice but could not see me.

"Yeah man, it's me. I sat on the edge of the bed and rested my hand on his shoulder. His eyes changed as if the awareness of another human being had pulled him to reality. Then, after a brief alertness, he returned into a stupor but attempted to speak.

"Man, I'm so glad you came. I love you man I love you so sorry I'm so sorry." He nodded off and then lifted his head up again. His face was terribly sad. "I'm sorry I want to be OK you hear this Tool song playing yeah I love this song man thanks I love you Josh you're my brother we're brothers I didn't mean to hurt you or anybody I'll be OK I'm gonna get better a better life it hurts your help it's like we share a soul you and me listen this is the best part the drum breakdown yeah listen to that they're so fucking awesome music I can make music like that my band I'll get better and we'll record I'll get a studio my band thank you for coming so much I knew you would brother."

I sat at the edge of the bed almost in tears. Only in movies had I witnessed a drug withdrawal and though I believed TV exaggerated everything, the pain and suffering of a real withdrawal, especially a family member, could never be acted out or exaggerated. Probably not even aware of what he told me, my brother began describing lucid tales of drug use, mostly nonsensical, every word making my skin crawl. In the back of my mind I had known he was in bad shape for a long time. Where had I been when he made the leap from marijuana and ecstasy to using heroin?

Jeremy continued talking mindlessly all night; he nodded off, slept, woke up screaming, threw up, sleepwalked and remained in a near comatose state for the next two days. My baby brother was a junkie. As my dreams of us growing old together with our families were questioned, I prayed to a God I rarely called upon anymore and I begged for help.

XIV

Too far gone. Slavery of the mind, the soul. Robbed of identity the individual lies, cheats and steals. He is stripped of rationalization, loses all pride and self-respect, acts upon the many evil and twisted thoughts normally locked deep within the mind. In the extreme, relationships are destroyed, bridges are burned, and ultimately the individual ends up alone, or perhaps only with other users who in a sense share a single moral code, but easily turn on each other for a quick high.

The world of a user exists so very far outside the conventional monotony and time-controlled reality of the normal, pedestrian life. Feelings and emotions are never fully understood except by those who live inside the culture, indifferent to schedules, social norms and values; trapped in oblivion. Those of us who live outside, we watch, beg them to get help, to get better, as if it can be done instantly. We have seen it done before. We know it is possible. Yet our naïve understanding never allows us to fully grasp the mindset, the psychology, the constant craving, the addictive personality of an addict.

For several months, Jeremy seemed to follow the straight and narrow. Having lost his previous job, he found one at another pizza place and soon became manager thanks to past experience, ingenuity, and constant hard work. Working hard never bothered him. In fact, it tended to keep him safe, away from trouble. *Idle hands do the devil's work.*

"If I don't get rich making music, then I want to own a restaurant. I got a name for it and everything. Munchie's. I got a bunch of ideas for the menu too." After quitting drugs, his energy appeared full throttle, his ideas worth a fortune if he could organize and put them into practice. Many an afternoon or evening, he cooked up some of his tasty recipes for the family and I to taste.

He and his band found a new singer, this time calling themselves Officer Down. The name represented a stand against authority. Every member except the drummer had been in jail or in trouble with the law for something. On stage, the guitar player and singer often burned the American flag or made slurs against the government and the police. It was freedom of speech at its finest.

The band found an old, isolated warehouse in a

shady part of town. It was the perfect spot to get away with almost anything they wanted. Located on Brooks Rd., it was on a street infamous for sleazy shake joints that ran along in spurts, unrespectable but still privately visited by those who held it publicly in low esteem. Police often patrolled the area, but rarely if ever searched the side streets where many older buildings were located, assuming no human activity took place at night.

"The Temple. We decided to call this place The Temple. What'd you think?"

"I like it. I like it." I told the truth and genuinely hoped the best.

Upon my first visit I noticed younger, mostly teenage guys and girls. They sat around drinking cheap beer in quart bottles and blowing cigarette and pot smoke into the already thick air. In small groups with brash attitudes, they were acutely aware of every movement from every other person in the place. Their eyes showed the natural teenage diffidence, the superficial need for acceptance and recognition. Like a dramatic movie, they played their parts. Every action performed and every sentence uttered was premeditated, hoping it would be cool, hoping it might get attention, hoping it might make them a unique individual.

The better looking girls dressed up like they were going to a dance club; tight, black stretch pants with short halter tops exposing their almost fully developed breasts and belly buttons, some with piercings or even tattoos unknown to their parents. The other girls who didn't quite have the bodies to wear these types of clothes adhered to their own style. They wore baggy pants, oversized T-shirts and usually dark makeup. Often, they stared jealously at the better looking girls, many obsessing to the point that they thought of nothing else all night, at the age of entering a world where looks seemed to mean so much.

Naturally, I caught myself staring at the pretty girls, still so young, fresh and somewhat innocent. A man will always recognize beauty. Age and human laws may dictate appropriate behavior but they fail to dictate desire. Besides, I was still young myself, over eighteen, but far from the age where I became that creepy old man who always gawked at the underage girls.

Still, I felt older. I dressed differently, more conservative. The once in-style fads and name brand clothes had given way to my own personal style, without regard to what the younger generation thought or wore.

I wasn't alone though. Many of my friends came along, and even parents of the band members showed up.

The band promised the owner that the space would be used only for practice, not to throw parties, not to sleep in, and definitely not to allow underage kids to drink and sell drugs. The oath had probably been broken the first night, but it wasn't likely the owner would show up on a weekend. More than a practice space, the band intended the warehouse to be a profitable moneymaker.

The blaring music in the background overpowered every attempt at holding a conversation. It was heavy, bearing all the weight of a generation angry at conventionality and authority. Or perhaps its ultimate purpose allowed a healthy, cathartic release of energy for my brother's age group. Whichever, they put their soul into the music they played like true musicians.

In the corner of the largest room of the building they played. A hall led to a few other rooms in the back, one used for a small studio, one for the 'backstage' area, where only the privileged were allowed to hang out with the band. This was where the groupies came after the show and during breaks. Those not invited were dealt a blow to their self-esteem.

"Mind if come back there?" I asked. Really, I just wanted to see what they were doing. I had become paranoid and skeptical about my brother since I found out he was a heroin user. Though I suspected he had not quit using for very long, I hoped and thought that maybe he would at least slow down or quit while I was around.

"Uh, I guess so. Come on back." Mike, the guitar player appeared reluctant and then loudly announced as if to warn everyone of my presence, "Hey Jeremy, you're brother's here."

Jeremy turned around quickly and a few others walked hastily in opposite directions, obviously with something too explicit for my eyes.

"Hey bro. You havin' fun?" He looked nervous. Sweat covered his head. His eyes were widely dilated.

"Definitely. So this is the backstage area, huh? This where ya'll bring all the females?"

"You know it." He just sort of sat there and stared with not much to say, anxious, like he had to be somewhere. Then, he got the excuse he wanted.

"Jeremy, you comin' or what?" A white guy with long brown dreadlocks stood at the outside door.

"Gotta go. You're gonna be here for a while right?"

"Yeah, yeah. I'll be here."

"Cool. We'll be right back. I'm gonna run to the store to grab some papers. Then we're gonna play again. I'll see ya."

Throughout the evening, the crowd came and went, slowly receding little by little. Many of the younger kids likely had curfews, going home drunk and high to greet their parents. I wondered how many would get in trouble. I wondered if their parents would know or even care for that matter.

The band played on and off into the late night. Jeremy stared blankly at the remaining crowd with a sense of wonder and satisfaction. In his mind, it was he the people had come to see. He was never happier than when he was playing music, especially on stage in front of people.

Yet something in his demeanor was different than I had seen in the past. The look of his childhood innocence was gone. His eyes were older, older than mine even, like he had already lived a full life. They had a desperate look, as if his dreams still existed, but were so much farther than before and steadily slipping farther, almost as if something in life had conquered them.

No doubt he was on some type of drug while on stage. The night progressed, and he zoned further out into his own world. He ignored those around him. By the time the family had left and only a few people remained, his mind was as gone as they were but in a different manner, a manner further nullifying his dreams and hopes.

Maybe I stuck around to watch the band. Maybe I stuck around hoping to take a girl home. Most likely, I stayed to keep an eye on my brother, all in vain. *"Am I my brother's keeper?"* I thought. No way could I keep an eye on him 24/7. Even when I was here with him, within feet, within talking distance, I still failed to stop him from using. What good was I as a brother? What good was I as a friend?

Jeremy didn't bother to say "bye" that night. I walked outside to where I had seen his girlfriend passed out in the car earlier. She still lay there, oblivious to the surrounding and ongoing rabble. When I tried to wake her up to see if Jeremy was still around, it was pointless. After searching further, I realized he was gone. He had left her there in the truck, passed out, in the middle of one of the worst parts of town, expecting someone else to care for her. He had probably gone to find more drugs.

XV

Junkies poured haphazardly and excitedly into the methadone clinic during the early morning to get their daily dosage. None looked especially happy, but all appeared overtly eager. Their movements were spastic and uncoordinated, their eyes empty and disengaged from any cognizant level of normal life. Many smoked cigarettes ravenously and talked obnoxiously while others coyly avoided any human contact like a beaten dog. I wondered how any of them functioned in society or if they held a regular job.

Early morning and still half asleep, I decided to venture into the building. I hoped to learn something that might help me understand better, help me stop being so judgmental towards my family, especially Jeremy. If he needed methadone to stay off drugs, then more power to him. I never fully understood how a government approved, synthetic form of heroin kept druggies from using, but I wanted nothing more than to believe it helped.

Years earlier, I had taken mother to the same spot on a few occasions. Usually I stayed in the car, ashamed someone might recognize me. I looked down on junkies, including mother, thinking they were weak minded and ignorant.

"What a waste of space. Maybe they'd all be better off dead. They're fucking miserable, the way they have to depend on that shit everyday. They should do to these people what they did the opium addicts in China – shoot 'em all."

Even with mother needing methadone, these were my feelings. Now, with my brother making six trips a week to the same clinic, I was confused. He was so young, and still I had the hope that these days would pass like a bad dream. Jeremy would get his life together and never touch drugs again.

The converted office space smelled like Lysol, reminiscent of a cheap motel room. Metal folding chairs left marks on the unswept supermarket-like tile floors. Pamphlets with bus schedules, NA meetings, AIDS, and hepatitis information filled a rack against the wall. To my surprise, several kids were sitting in a corner playing with toys.

"Who would bring their kids to a place like this?" I felt sorry for the children and especially for their future. Jeremy looked at me and knew exactly what I

was thinking.

"Crazy, huh?"

"Definitely."

"I think I have to see my counselor today and maybe take a piss test. If I pass, then they'll give me carry-outs and lower my dosage. I won't have to come but three days a week then."

"Good, good." I attempted to sound happy, as if he had accomplished something spectacular. In all honestly, the fact that he depended on this shit made me ill.

Weeks earlier, when summer was near, I had planned another road trip, one that would not be as long because now I had a serious girlfriend and Jeremy and I could not depend on our grandmother anymore for money. Between father and my brother, she was wiped out. Still, I had saved money and figured Jeremy could come up with at least enough to take a weeklong trip, possibly a few days more.

"Man, I should have told you this, but I was using again and I figured if I got on methadone it might help me quit. So far it has." The look in his eyes told me he was lying. "I don't plan on needing it for very long, but right now I got to go to the clinic everyday except

Sunday."

"Oh, OK." I was at a loss for words. "Honestly, I knew you were using again. It was obvious, avoiding me, acting funny when I'm around. Your eyes give it away a lot of times. It's to the point where I can just tell, you know?"

"Yeah, I figured you knew. But I'm tryin' to get clean, I promise. I guess I couldn't do it on my own the first time like I thought I could. But maybe the methadone will help."

"I hope so. I guess this means no trip though, huh?"

"Maybe by the end of the summer we can go. If I do real well then they'll give me carry-outs and we can at least go for a few days somewhere."

"Yeah, yeah, OK. That's better than nothing. I'd like to do something this summer, just the two of us."

"Me too bro, me too."

So here, already near the end of the summer, I waited as patiently as possible in the clinic while Jeremy met with his counselor and took the piss test. I sat quietly, studying the people, listening to their conversations about nothing important. Most patients were white and of every age group. The younger ones seemed to have already lived full lives, only recently trapped by the spell of drugs, still new to the game, yet far from naive and innocent. Their eyes showed sadness and regret, their youthful vitality zapped. They hated being at the clinic and wanted nothing more than for the methadone to work. Older patients looked badly worn from years of self-abuse.

"Jesus." I said to myself. *"How long have they been on this shit?"* Women with scarred-up arms and men skinnier than a rail waited fervently for their dose, some with small lunchboxes with locks. I surmised the boxes were for the veteran methadone users to carry their doses home for the week. Too early in the morning for me to be awake, I paced around the clinic, read the pamphlets and wondered if my brother had contracted hepatitis or even HIV. The thought was disturbing.

I promised to help out Jeremy any way I could. At present, he owned no vehicle. In fact, he had gone through at least three in the past year. Two my grandfather had signed for and put up the down payment. Jeremy wrecked both within a month. He was lucky to be alive, a cat with nine lives and using them up quickly. What happened to the other vehicle I could not say, whether it was repossessed, traded for drugs, or stolen.

"Hey bro, you ready? You look bored?" Jeremy walked out from the back room.

"I'm fine. Gettin' educated. Reading up on things over here. You get tested for this stuff?" I pointed at the pamphlet on HIV.

"Yeah, they actually test us up here. Negative, everything's negative."

"Thank god for that. You ever share needles?" All of a sudden I had twenty questions to ask.

"No, never done that. Always used my own."

"Good, good." I had no idea of knowing if he was telling the truth. After looking in his eyes so many times, sometimes I thought I knew and every time I wanted to believe him. But methadone, like the other drugs, gave his eyes that blank stare, glassy and out of touch with reality. It made it that much harder to see the truth and to know the person Jeremy had become.

"So when you take that stuff it completely makes you stay away from other drugs or what? I don't understand?" I continued my questioning as we got into the car.

"Well, not really. It makes the craving for opiates supposedly disappear. When you do them you don't feel anything. So what's the point, right?"

"What about everything else?"

"Nope, doesn't really affect those much. Cocaine, crack, anything that makes you speed. Doesn't work against them."

"So you could do methadone and crack and still feel both? Most addicts will take whatever drug they can get anyway, won't they? I don't see the fucking point."

"Maybe. It keeps a lot of people off the heroin though. The other drugs just don't feel the same either."

"Speaking of which, are we going on our road trip or what? Did you pass the piss test?"

"Fuckin' pot was in my system, but that's it. I was going to use some of grandma's piss, but the dude was watching me too close. Fucking sucks, don't it? Now they won't give me my carry-outs." He stared out the window, not upset because he failed the test, but because the counselor was doing his job.

"Sorry bro. I was lookin' so forward to this trip too. It's been awhile since I been anywhere really. Next summer we'll take a big trip somewhere. I'll have a good job by then and save plenty of money."

XVI

"Calm down, calm down. I can barely understand you. Jeremy did what now?"

My grandmother cried unintelligibly over the phone, speaking about another wrong my brother committed against her. He had gone over the edge. Antiques, tools and even jewelry mysteriously disappeared from the houses of grandmother and stepmother. Jeremy was banned from stepmother's unless she was there, and even then he wasn't exactly welcome. My grandmother refused to believe he was capable of such atrocities, and now she was hysterical with disbelief and heartache.

"Are you sure? How much? What? Look, I'll call the girl at the bank and tell her your checks are missing. No, I won't say he took them. What do you mean you aren't sure it's him? You just told me it was him. No, I'm not going to hurt him grandma. He needs to be in jail is where he needs to be. Things are coming up missing all the time. If I were you I would press charges. I know you won't but it may be the only way to save him from himself."

My fists were clenched as I paced the empty classroom at school. Lunchtime would be over in minutes, and I would need to forget about Jeremy, at least temporarily. The rest of the day would pass slowly. Any small infraction by a student and I would snap, taking out my anger at the kids. Or I would remain perfectly calm, superficially happy with a smile on my face, as if the world were perfect. It was a coping mechanism I used to deal with the constant chaos of my life, one I had learned as a child.

"I promise. I'll call you after school and let you know what the bank said. I gotta go. Love you too. Bye."

Searching around the room for something to throw, the bell for sixth period rang. I wasn't about to throw my cell phone again. Already, I had destroyed two others because of my anger towards Jeremy. This time was the last straw. Grandmother's checks were missing, and over two hundred dollars had been taken from her account. Jeremy was the last around and though she didn't want to believe him guilty, she finally called me because she figured only I could put a stop to it.

School could not end quickly enough. Within

seconds after the last bell, I was out of the door to beat the traffic. I raced to my brother's apartment with every intention of breaking my promise to grandmother.

"I'm not gonna hurt him," I had promised. It was a lie. So many times in the recent past I had wanted to beat his ass. Not that it would help any, but stealing from the family and even from me? This wasn't the brother I had grown up with; the one I shared everything with, the one who I believed had such a bright future and had such great talent. Now his mind was burnt out, completely altered and seemingly beyond redemption.

In fifteen minutes, I had driven almost thirty miles and my anger only grew. I ran to the door with my heart still pumping full blast and knocked gently. No answer. I dared not yell because if he heard the rage in my voice, I knew he would not answer. Finally, after knocking five minutes or more, the door slowly came open. Jeremy peeked around the corner, eyes asleep, the room completely dark, though the day was sunny and bright.

I said nothing. I pushed open the door with force, almost knocking Jeremy down. He looked surprised, as if the thought of me doing such a thing never crossed his mind.

"What the fuck are you thinking? Stealing from

grandma?" He remained silent. Without hesitation I punched him in the nose. The blood began to run immediately down his surprised face and he attempted to escape into another room. I followed him, but could not bring myself to hit him again. He looked not scared, but incredibly astonished.

Already I was ashamed of myself, yet at the same time felt he deserved it.

"Why? Why did you do it?" I yelled as I approached him. He couldn't bring himself to answer. He just looked at me startled, fully aware under his drugged stupor of the significance of this imminent encounter. Somewhere along the path of life our bond had fallen apart. Now, it was completely severed. Though extrinsically I attributed all of it to his addiction, somewhere deep inside I felt partly responsible. Not because I had done drugs with him in the past, but because I had abandoned him in a sense, hadn't I? I had become judgmental rather than understanding. I had wanted so badly to escape, to stay away from those demons possessing my family, that in the process of focusing on my own life, I had let him deteriorate. I was his older brother. Wasn't it partly my fault?

I left him there, still bloody, burning a hole

through me with his ghostly stare.

"It happens again and I'll fuck you up. I promise."
He remained silent and held his nose.

As I walked to the car and slammed the door, I
began to cry. My brother's pain was my pain, ounce for
ounce. Life could never be happy or complete unless he
was there to share it with me. I drove around for a few
hours, recollecting, crying, yelling and cursing everyone
from my parents to god. What my family did to deserve
such a curse I didn't know. After the swelling in my
eyes was gone and I looked somewhat normal again, I
went home to my girlfriend and put on my smiley face.
She never knew anything was wrong.

XVII

My brother spent a full month inside the jail at 201
Poplar before I decided to visit. Certainly he needed to
be taught a lesson, but somewhere deep within me a tiny
bit of sympathy existed, a hope that maybe jail time
would give him a wake-up call, help him turn around his
life. These years, his early twenties, were supposed to
be his prime. Yet instead of living them to the fullest,
he was wasting away in a jail cell, not for robbing my
grandmother or another member of the family, but for
stealing from his job at the pizza place.

After realizing the nightly deposit had not been
made, the owner rushed to the store one morning only to
find that it was still closed. Jeremy had failed to show
up for his regular morning shift. With money missing,
the police were called, my brother was accused, and
suddenly he was a fugitive. Already his drug problem
had cost him his apartment. He moved back in with
mother. When the police finally caught him he was
hiding in her attic. She was almost taken to jail as well
for denying that he was there.

"I.D," the overweight black woman who guarded

the entrance demanded rather than asked. I took out my license.

"Who you here for?" The woman had a serious and demeaning face, as if she possessed some sort of superior air because she was a prison guard.

"My brother, Jeremy Savage."

She stared hard at my license and then returned it. She waved me through apathetically and moved on to the next person.

I emptied the change and the keys from my pockets and walked through the metal detectors. The waiting room had the brutal, hot, stuffy scent of a crowd of people. Rows of cheap metal chairs attached to each other and to the ground were almost full. The crowd was mostly black save a few Hispanics. Only one other white woman, easily discernable against the dark faces, sat alone quietly.

Young girls, still children themselves, definitely too young to be mothers, held babies that their fathers had probably never seen on the outside. The babies had no business in this environment, no business in the world really, exposed to this type of life so early and more than likely destined for failure. Looking around one felt an overwhelming pessimism at the whole world in general. With so many humans on this earth, living in these conditions, walking around, ignorant and knowing no other way, it was easy to want to just give up and say fuck it. What could one do to change anything?

Voices penetrated the air loudly and obnoxiously while others sat ambivalently staring at the floor or at others, analyzing or envying them. No one appeared happy. Coming from work, I still wore my dress clothes. Everyone glanced at me and then looked away. I felt a timid arrogance but knew I was no better than anyone in the room. True, maybe they lived in the ghetto, maybe they had children at a young age and spent more money on hair weave than child rearing, maybe they were criminals or on drugs, but here we were all equal. Here we were powerless against the law, against the cocky police officers who could not look or talk to us without condescendence. We all had family or friends who were criminals and locked up.

Anxiously playing with the piece of paper that contained a number, I glanced from person to person. I prayed no one would recognize me and vice versa. I stared at the few good looking girls, watching their asses as they walked by, wondering if they were easy, undressing them in my head. Surely if they were here,

they were easy. These thoughts crossed my mind, one
of the many assumptions I made as I judged and waited.

An hour later, my number was called. I looked at
the piece of paper, now worn to a thin and sweaty pulp,
and walked to the counter. I signed my name. Walking
towards where the inmates awaited their visitors, I
stopped at the bathroom to wash my clammy hands and
splash cold water over my face. I wanted to appear as
calm and together as possible.

Upstairs, two rooms, each with two long rows of
booths contained phones attached to the walls. Both the
walls and the phones were smudged with years of dirt
and other human build-up, gritty and filthy. A thick,
unbreakable glass separated visitors from inmates. I
searched for a booth away from the more crowded areas,
immediately giving up on finding a clean one. Everyone
attempted to talk above everyone else. No privacy
existed and no one seemed to care. While I waited for
Jeremy I heard everything from "I miss you" to "you
need to find a way to pay the light bill, nigga."

There were tears behind some glass and rage
behind others. A big girl, 200 lbs. minimum, began a
strip tease in front of her incarcerated man. She pulled
her shirt up and exposed her bra that barely held her

saggy breasts. Probably no one on our side of the glass could see except me, and from where I sat I saw every roll of her stomach. She noticed and smiled my way, not missing a pause. Her man laughed.

Jeremy finally appeared dressed in a navy blue jumpsuit. His hair was long and shaggy and he looked as if he had not shaven in weeks. The house shoes he wore had holes. His face looked sad as he feigned a faint smile. He was happy to see me but ashamed as well. He seemed drugged up, a little sluggish and uncoordinated. Never had I seen him look so rough. The only positive thing I noticed was that he had put back on some weight, so at least he was eating.

We picked up the receiver simultaneously. We had to tilt our necks and raise our heads to the phone at an uncomfortable angle to hear each other speak.

"Hey bro. You finally came."

"Yeah. Probably should have come earlier but I've been busy."

"Yeah. I hear ya." An uncomfortable minute passed with complete silence. A slight feeling of guilt came over me for not visiting before. "You been doing alright?" Jeremy broke the ice.

"Yeah, yeah. Same old thing. Working. Staying

busy." Words were difficult to find.

"How's your girl?"

"Good, good. How 'bout you? You making it OK in this place?"

"The best I can. I mean it fuckin' sucks ya know, but I guess I did it to myself. I think I'll get out of here in about two more weeks though. Got a court date on the eighteenth."

"Good, good. So what's it like here? Anything like they show on TV? Fighting all the time and gangs and all that shit?"

"Yeah, a little. I see fights all the time. This one guy got his eye poked out the other day. It was fuckin' crazy." For such a dramatic incident, he told the story with little expression or emotion.

"Damn. Are you serious? Has anyone bothered you?"

"No, not really. They think I'm crazy. I always walk around talking to myself and singing Tool. I go see the psychiatrist every week."

"You keep doin' that and they may send you to a crazy house instead."

"Fine with me. Anything is better than this shit-hole. I just want to get the fuck out. I'd love to have a fuckin' Coke and a cigarette right now."

"They don't allow Cokes or anything, huh?"

"Nope. I mean, some people smoke, but if the guards catch you, it's an extra week for each time. It ain't worth it. You can get most anything you want in here really. But me, all I want is out of this place. I'm not messin' around with none of that shit anymore."

My heart dropped. Once again I knew he was lying and that even a stint in jail might not save him. He was on some type of drug as we spoke. Maybe he believed what he said and failed to grasp his own self-destructive reality. Maybe he was trapped in his own twisted state of mind.

"What about the methadone and stuff. Wasn't it hard to come down off that?"

"Yeah. It hurt. Bad. I thought I was gonna die for a couple of days. They gave me pills to help me come off of it a little. I was throwing up in the cell, crying, yelling."

"Are you still taking the pills?"

"Some. Not as much as before." We sat in silence. He knew what I was thinking. His tired and dreary eyes opened and closed. His head nodded a few times. Then suddenly, like he received an injection of adrenaline, he said,

"Man, Josh. I can't live like this anymore. I gotta do right. Please help me do right. I'm sorry for everything. You know I don't want to hurt anyone, especially my family." His head fell and rested against the glass.

"Just get through this. Hopefully you'll be out soon and you can start fresh. Find a new job, get your life back on track…"

"Will you help me?"

"Of course I will. I'll do whatever I can. You just have to stay off the drugs." I said it like it was easy to do. "That's the main cause of all your problems. You have so much talent, so much energy."

"I know, I know. It's ruining my life."

The lights flickered several times and I could faintly hear a voice yelling on Jeremy's side of the glass. He looked towards the voice.

"It's time to go. We only get thirty minutes. Less by the time we walk over here. I love you bro. Tell the family 'hey' and 'I love them'. Come see me again if you can. Hopefully I'll be out soon before you get the chance to." He stuck his fist to the glass. I put mine to his.

"Love you too bro. Don't worry. You'll be out soon and all this will be over." His eyes teared up as he walked away. He spent another month in jail. I visited again the next week. I brought my parents and grandmother with me.

XVIII

An unexpected letter arrived in the mail from the city of Memphis. Scared to open it, I walked slowly inside the house, wondering what it could possibly say. *"Have I forgotten to pay a ticket? I don't remember getting one recently."* My driving record wasn't exactly spotless, but after my insurance skyrocketed and I bought a new vehicle, I drove more carefully. Nearly three years had passed since my last traffic ticket.

Once inside the house, I opened the letter. A notice informed me that my driver's license would be suspended within the next two weeks if I failed to pay a fine of almost two hundred dollars.

"What the fuck?" I yelled. No one was there to hear me. "Why the hell do I owe this?" I examined the notice more closely. I read the date. Not familiar. I read the tag number. Even less familiar. I searched for the type of vehicle. A green Chevrolet. *"Who the hell drives a green Chevrolet?"* For the life of me, I could not think because of my anger. *"A green Chevrolet, a green Chevrolet...* Mother Fucker! That's my dad's car. I've never driven his car. There's no fuckin' way I could have gotten this… Wait a minute." I examined the notice again. No driver's license number appeared, only my social security number.

"That fuckin' punk. I can't believe he did this shit. I can't believe it."

By now, I was pacing the room, blood red in the face and indecisive about my next move.

"Should I call him? He won't answer. I just saw him a few days ago. He didn't say shit to me about this. Of course he wouldn't. It's got to be him. Who else could it be? Should I go ahead and call the police? Try to press charges? Dammit!" I yelled loudly.

I called mother. She seemed as surprised as me.

"Are you sure? No, he hasn't said anything. Your father lets him borrow the car all the time even though he knows he doesn't have a driver's license. The police have been by here several times to look for him in the last few weeks."

"Are you serious? What did he do now?" I asked.

"He says his parole officer violated him for no reason. He says she's racist. I don't know what's going on with him half the time. He does really well for a while and then…"

"That's why he's using my name. He doesn't

want to go to jail again. Dammit! Now I'm about to lose my license or have to pay a huge fine because of that sorry ass fucker."

"Call and tell them what happened. Maybe you can sort it out."

"Just tell him to call me when he gets there." I hung up the phone. Still pacing violently around the house, I called the number on the bottom of the notice. Busy. I waited about thirty seconds. Busy again. Another thirty seconds. Still busy. Angrily, I threw the phone against the wall. It made a large hole and broke.

"Dammit!" No matter, I still had my cell. I had been thinking of getting rid of the landline anyway. Since I rarely used it, it was a waste of money. I called father.

"I don't know what you're talking about. I wasn't with him when he did it. Are you sure it was him? No, it wasn't me. How am I going to pass for a twenty-four year old? I wish. Well, I'll talk to him. He's got the car right now. No, I don't know where he is. I'll have him call you."

Father was lying. He always took up for Jeremy. Jeremy was father's favorite and I mother's, an obvious but unspoken truth proved only too often throughout our lives. I hung up and called the city again.

"Hello? Yes, I received a notice in the mail that my license would be suspended. Yes, I can hold." I still paced.

"Yes. The number of the citation? It's 06780871. OK. Yes. No, it's not me. I drive a blue Explorer. No, I've never driven a green Chevrolet. Do I know someone who does?" For a moment my anger turned into sympathy. *Should I tell them I know exactly who did this? Should I tell them my brother is responsible?* No, I have no idea. I just know it's not me. What? But I can't come down before that date, especially in the morning. I have a job. I work. There's no other way? I guess I have no choice then, do I? Whatever. Thanks a lot for your help."

The only way to resolve the matter was a trip downtown to speak first to a clerk and then to a judge. In order to do this I would have to miss a full day of work and get a letter from my principal stating that I was in school on the specific day and time that the ticket was issued. All this wasted time and effort to save my license. I was determined that my brother would go with me and confess. But first, he would confess to me. I wanted to hear his excuses, his probable lies, the reason he fucked me. What had I done to him?

Time has a way of subduing anger. Days passed. Weeks passed. The principal wrote me a letter. I went downtown and waited two or three hours to talk to a judge whose motto seemed to be 'guilty until proven innocent'. After harassing me with questions, she threw the ticket out. I wasn't charged a dime and my license was safe. Only my time was wasted.

Naturally, Jeremy did everything he could to avoid me. Though I wanted a reason and an apology, I already knew the answer. He was scared of returning to jail. I truly believed that it was nothing personal against me. It just happened to be my Social Security number he told the officer. He had memorized it years ago when I gave him an extra ID before he turned eighteen. Now, well past eighteen, he remained a frightened little child hiding behind whatever could save him. Still so immature and seemingly stuck that way, drugs had stunted his mindset, his maturity. The more he used, the more he regressed. He was bringing down the family as well.

I finally caught Jeremy at mother's one day. He heard me drive up and bolted upstairs. Mother told me where he was. I climbed the stairs.

"Josh, don't do anything to him. Please. He's still your brother."

I ignored her. Part of me wanted to fight. Part of me wanted to hug him. I opened the door. He sat on the bed, pretending to be surprised, his eyes fearful.

"Hey man. What's up?" I said nothing.

"Man, I'm sorry. For real. I don't know what to say. I'll go down there with you if you want and turn myself in. I don't want you to get in trouble." I was tempted take him up on the offer just to see if he would actually do it.

"It' been taken care of. I spent four fuckin' hours at 201 sorting it out. I didn't tell them it was you, but they looked up the tags. They'll probably figure it out."

"It was only one time. I won't let it happen again. I promise. I haven't been driving much. I'm just scared to go back to jail, you know? I hate that place."

"I can imagine. Why the hell won't you act right? What did you do, skip a probation meeting?"

"It's not my fault. It's the probation officer. She's got it out for me 'cause I'm white. I'm tellin' you, she's racist. I called her and told her I didn't have a ride to the meeting and she said she'd reschedule. So I ask her

when it is and she says she'll call me. A week later I
call her to ask again and she says she's already violated
me because I missed it. And on top of that, she says my
piss tested positive for cocaine which is impossible
because I used grandma's piss."

"What the fuck?" I was surprised of what I heard
even though I had heard it before. "I don't care if she is
racist. You're fucking stupid if you think you can
bullshit your way through life this way. When are you
going to grow up? They put people on probation for a
reason, you know? Because they're usually criminals.
You're a fuckin' criminal. If you're doing what you're
supposed to, why the hell would you have to use
grandma's piss anyway? Maybe you need to be in jail.
It might save your life."

"What the fuck ever man. I don't need to listen to
your shit. Always judging me. You always got the
answer don't ya, like everything is so easy, like your
way is the only way. You don't understand shit.
Everybody lets you take care of everything. What about
me? What the fuck do I get? Huh?"

"What the hell are you talking about? If I get
anything, it's because I've been responsible. I'm not
throwing my fuckin' life away on drugs. You think I

want the burden of being the responsible one? You
think it's easy? It's easier to take your way out and just
say fuck it, let me stay high all the time, let me live off
my mom, let me not give a shit about anybody but
myself."

"Fuck you. That's not the way I feel."

"Oh really? Maybe you've just fried your brain.
You can't even think straight anymore. Look at you.
Look at your arms." I grabbed one and held it up.
Small purple dots where needles were used covered his
arm. He pulled away and tried to leave the room.

"That's it, walk away. I tell you what though. If
you use my name again I promise I'll kick your ass and
press charges. That's fucked up to do to me and you
know it."

The front door slammed loudly. With no car, no
phone and probably no money, he had no place to go so
he began walking aimlessly down the street.

"What happened?" Mother asked.

"What do you think happened? He never wants to
face up to anything, same as always. He'll be back in
jail before too long. Probably the best thing for him. At
least there he can't fuck up the people's life around
him."

Jeremy ran from the law for another two months. By the time he was arrested I had at least five traffic tickets in three different vehicles. At least two more days I missed school and spent the day at 201 Poplar attempting to clear my name. I was fingerprinted, had to sign my name several times to check it against signatures on the tickets, and I went before the judge and the district attorney before they suspiciously cleared my name. Suspiciously because they suspected that I knew the person causing me these problems. Still, even after everything my brother had done, I could not bring myself to tell them that Jeremy Savage, my little brother, was the person guilty of using my identity to save himself from returning to prison.

XIX

Life is difficult for the junkie. Most people are quick to judge and say that the blame is his own, that the junkie puts himself in such a predicament. They would be right in saying so. Yet, even when a junkie tries to go straight, the world remains against him, especially a long time junkie, or one with a criminal record. Few if any businesses will hire him. Without a license or transportation, the world becomes even colder and harsher. If he does find a job it will be low-paying, degrading, and monotonous work. The walk to the bus stop and back everyday will add hours to his already long day. The rainy and cold days will beat him down until he is ready to give up or begin using again, depressed with the world against him. When he calls friends and family and wants to hang out or ask a favor, he often finds only mistrust and avoidance.

So many junkies are good people deep down, talented in some manner such as the arts or possessing some other special gift absent in most normal people. They often see reality in a different light, outside of the box and with unique vision. Most experiment with drugs, never imagining that one day they will lose all dignity and self-respect, not to mention jobs, friends, relationships, and every other aspect of typical everyday life. The high no longer appears worth it all. But by then it is too late, the body is physically and mentally addicted and only the high can offer them any opportunity of feeling good. Only it can make them forget their pain and the pain they have caused others. And if they once used the expensive drugs like heroin or cocaine, by now they cannot afford those and they get high on whatever they can find, often resorting to crime. Only a small part of humanity remains as they deteriorate, slowly leeching on society, giving us more reason to hate them. And so the cycle continues...

XX

"Yeah bro, I'm proud of you. For real. I was beginning to wonder if you ever gonna straighten up." Jeremy and I passed the day lazily away. We slept until 11 am after watching movies all night. Then we ate cereal for breakfast while watching another bootleg DVD. Later in the day we played catch with the football. When we became bored we searched for small stones in the back yard to use with the slingshot.

"I know. I know. I just can't live like that anymore. I've hurt too many people. You, grandma, my friends…"

"The important thing is that you're doing well now. And as long as you're trying, I'll help the best I can."

Jeremy had spent over six months in jail. With the many missed court dates, the accumulated traffic tickets, and the original charges of theft, the judge wanted to make an example of him.

"I had a lot of time in there to think you know, a lot of time to write. I wrote stories about the inside, stories about us when we were little, lyrics for songs. I wrote letters just about everyday to the family. I studied for my GED. I didn't have my guitar so I had to do something to keep myself occupied or else I would've gone crazy."

"I bet. You could probably write a book on everything you saw in there."

"For sure."

Time again subdued my anger about the traffic tickets. I felt so sorry for my brother sitting in prison that I had to visit. His letters containing countless apologies and newfound hopes for redemption brought tears to my eyes. No matter what he had done in the past, I was always willing to forgive him.

A hummingbird appeared and started to drink the sweet red water my girlfriend had mixed and put in the bird feeder. Jeremy and I stood still in the backyard watching.

"Isn't it cool how their wings move so fast you can't even see them? Such small creatures." I aimed at the nearby limb where another bird rested. The rock hit the exact spot but the bird was already gone.

"Quick too."

"Your turn." I handed him the slingshot and searched for more good stones.

After Jeremy was released from prison I offered him a place to stay, free of charge, at least until he got back on his feet. In all honesty I didn't really think he would take my offer, especially after refusing so many times before, but I was glad he did. On top of that, he was attending GED classes at the nearby college. His entire outlook on life had seemed to genuinely change.

"I hope there's some good lookin' females in class tonight. Last week it was just me and this big black chic. I mean, you know it's been awhile and all, but I ain't goin' there. Not yet anyway." He chuckled. "So, you'll pick me up at eight, right?"

"A little after. As soon as *The Office* is over I'll leave the house. Niki should have dinner ready by then."

"Hell ya. That girl can cook. I know why you keep her around. See ya soon." Jeremy shut the car door and walked excitedly to class.

I watched as he entered the building, happier than I had been in a long time. Whenever I made a wish, whether throwing a coin in a fountain, witnessing a falling star, or noticing the clock hitting 11:11, I wished that my brother would straighten his life up. Maybe, finally, those countless wishes had not been wasted.

It must have been the boredom that killed him. The regular life most of us live, the forty-hour week, the regular job, normalcy, without the drama and perpetual chaos that some people need. Others thrive from it.

Jeremy didn't stay with me long. Without a job he somehow rented an apartment. Soon he was buying new music equipment, furniture, clothing, plus he had extra money to blow. Naturally the GED was the last thing on his mind, but he appeared happy. After so long in the dumps, his self-esteem was improving. He played music and dated girls again. Jail time and heroin had killed his self-esteem, not to mention his libido. Seeing him in such high spirits for the first time in a long while, the last thing I wanted to do was criticize.

"Whatever you're doing, just be careful. If you get busted, you'll be in jail a long time."

"I know. Besides, I'm not going to do it very long. Just enough to get back on my feet."

My brother lived from one extreme to the other. No in-between, no middle ground existed. Either he was strung out and could barely function in society or he was straight and making a shitload of cash with some scheme. This time he was stealing copper from old abandoned buildings, large businesses and warehouses.

"This shit is worth a fortune right now. You know copper was the first metal ever used by humans? Read that in the history book you lent me. Yep, I'm still studying. Don't worry, bro. Still gonna get my GED."

Though against his actions, I realized by now that my pleading was futile and only drove him farther away.

"I've learned from my mistakes. All I have to do is stay off the drugs and I can make money quick, buy music equipment and studio time. When I do that, me and the band will record some tunes and hopefully get signed or at least get some gigs to make money. Then I won't need to do this shit anymore."

Was he really as naïve as he sounded or burnt-out from too many drugs? Maybe a combination of the two. Whatever the case, I subtly made comments here and there, all the while knowing he would eventually end up back in jail or worse, dead. He scared me to death.

"You know I saw on the news where they have been looking for people stealing copper, especially out of homes and people's air conditioning units."

"I wouldn't do that man, not from someone's house. That's mean." Or so he said.

Soon he had his hand in everything. Though I

wanted to hang out and keep him out of trouble, I was scared to even ride to the store with him. I had no idea what he was carrying, if he had another warrant, if someone was after him, if he was using a stolen or a fake credit card. On more than one occasion he had been beaten up or robbed at gunpoint. His excuses were always the same.

"I got jumped man. I was just walking late one night to the store to get some cigarettes and these guys jumped me."

Later he would tell me the truth, either forgetting he had lied or wanting to be honest during one of our heart to heart conversations over a beer. In reality a drug deal had gone bad in the wrong part of town or he didn't have enough money to pay a dealer. By now I had become passive and unwilling to share my true feelings. Deep down though, or when I was alone, my heart ached as I thought about how his vicious cycle continued spiraling out of control. Yet God was keeping him alive for a reason.

On his twenty-seventh birthday, I became more worried than ever. As long as I could remember, he had told me that twenty-seven would be the age of his death.

"I'm gonna die at the same age as Jimi Hendrix,

Kurt Cobain or one of those other bad ass musicians. I wanna fuckin' live crazy and die young. Fuck getting old. You see how pop and mom are. They can barely get around."

He hadn't mentioned this in a long while, not even when his birthday rolled around. Maybe he had forgotten. Maybe he had realized that the life of the rich and fabulous rock star that he had expected and wanted so badly had eluded him and faded away. Whatever the reason, I decided not to say anything until he turned twenty-eight, begging higher forces to make it past the year.

The closer it came, the more relived I felt, yet at the same time I watched him slowly slipping away. He started to take methadone again. I saw him less and less. Every time I went to his apartment, I saw drug paraphernalia strewn everywhere. Most of his new furniture and other newly purchased possessions slowly began to disappear. Months after he moved in, he had only a mattress in his bedroom, a small TV, and a couch. Everything else was old furniture he had cajoled from grandma or discovered on the side of the street.

XXI

Can't feel my hands numb going numb squeeze to feel
got to squeeze to feel breathing tough catch my breath in
out in out warped messed up emotions can't hide from
them want to cry can't let it out try to cry to yell to hit
something no don't break it tried that doesn't work well
what can I do maybe see a psychologist tell a friend no a
psychologist someone objective listener tell me the right
thing to do the right way to act some days I'm happy no
always sad just try to be happy pretend I can pretend
really well smile big smile I'm good at that no one
knows do they Do they know The eyes tell me they do
they know something maybe not everything maybe not
my pain but they know something is wrong my eyes are
sad my behavior erratic snap I snap at any second not
like before they feel the tension I see them looking
staring knowing I pray for the workday to be over to end
but in all honesty it's the only thing that keeps me going
keeps my mind off of my family my family so sad so
miserable my job keeps me sane a recess from the worry
must perform can't quit not now go I've gained so much
the day over soon the night no pain I can sleep six seven

hours longer Hopefully I love to sleep never wake up can I sleep and never wake up Oh god this is depression isn't it the condition doctors medicate for not me how got to get rid of this feeling let it go so easy right wrong loneliness emptiness pain damn it hurts so bad my chest tightening breath in out squeeze your fists numb no I'm OK I'll be fine pressure too much constantly sawing away at my mind my sanity can't get rid of this feeling dominate my thoughts damn periods of happiness overtaken by worries even those good moments in life that I am thankful for a beautiful girl a job I enjoy a car a house but family no family take them away let them die no love God my heart hurts so badly am I wrong should I stay away try to make something of myself at the risk of losing my family my family unhappy patience wait it out give in out of love what love take their route drown my worries with drugs medications less painful anything to diminish the pain my family doesn't seem to mind who they hurt in the process who they take advantage of as long as they stay high everything else falls in place life may be a daily struggle but at least they have each other to help where's my help certainly they would welcome me they love me don't they love me I love them I hate them I wish they would

die they have done me so wrong but we are family we
can forgive blood thicker than water deeper than roots
my brother he is my brother not the same as before gone
where did he go save him I want to save him to bring
him back what great things we could have accomplished
with his talent and my intelligence so close we are were
so close tight the wind blows and time passes the
seasons change and my family I'm losing time I need to
help I don't want to help Die! No don't say that help
them help my brother so far away from me my lifestyle
my mindset what I would do to bring him back sell my
soul possessions risk my future maybe that's it give up
everything one last try to save his soul we are one he
and I we are one soul share one life one soul
aaaahhhhh!!!!!! baby brother tears flow for your
recovery perhaps it is I who would give your world a
chance you have tried to live up to my standards to my
test tried to impress me and looked up to me throughout
your life and what have I done for you one last attempt
scared so scared what if I lose it all hope all progress
what if I lose my own soul will we be close again the
void empty it will be worth it souls together again cry I
cry there it goes again my heart heavy sinks in my chest
lay down I don't want to do anything really lay down

nothing don't want to cry don't want to feel don't want to watch TV don't want to read write nothing just sit and think don't want to think it hurts everything pointless life years from now no brother pointless empty feel empty sad I see a future without you sad so miserable bleak a void never filled something I can never fill or repair always wondering what could have been must try to reach you brother.

XXII

The impending pernicious night overwhelmed and refused to allow passivity to creep upon me. Through a complete silence, voices in my head argued back and forth, those of morality versus malice. While one spoke of the value of family, the other rationalized about the detrimental path I was determined to follow. Neither provided a clear solution to the inevitable.

No longer could I sit back and watch as my brother wasted away into oblivion. I needed to fully understand his addiction, his state of mind, his never-ending urge to always be high. Only then could I truly share his way of life and accept him for whom he was. I had to get high.

Maybe just once, maybe twice, whatever it took, I would be fine. Throughout our childhood and into adulthood I had always been the one who never had an 'addictive' personality.

"You're a one-percenter Josh," my mom explained bragging on me. "You're lucky you don't have that gene. You're like your grandfather. He didn't have it either. The doctor told him to quit smoking or it would catch up with him. That same day he went home and threw all his cigars out, just like that. Never smoked again." She always blamed it on genes, just like my dad always claimed his alcohol addiction was a disease.

"You don't understand, son. I hope you never will. It's like having cancer or AIDS. It's not so easy to just quit. We just have to take things one day at a time"

Likely story. By the time I was a teenager I was so tired of their AA and twelve-step bullshit that I swore I would never become an addict.

Still, every word stuck in my head. Getting high a few times wouldn't hurt. If I could just have the feeling a time or two, maybe I could comprehend it and then find a way out, a way to stop the urge for both my baby brother and me. And if nothing else, at least we would be close again. At least our bond would continue on and on like we promised each other so many times, like in the not so far gone past.

The clock read past midnight. Restless, I left the house determined to see my brother.

"He might still be awake, might even have some on him already, who knows? Don't have any idea how much that shit costs. Can't be cheap. That's OK, I brought money, cash. We'll get some if nothing else." I

talked to myself while driving, lost in thought, nervous and afraid, and thinking about turning back every second.

Jeremy's apartment building was located in a shady part of Memphis. Prostitutes who looked like women but had protruding Adam's apples strolled the nearby streets on warm nights. Drug dealers hid in shadows throughout the neighborhood. A methadone clinic conveniently sat right next door to his building. Yet instead of the run down crack house one might expect, the apartment complex was well kept and occupied by paying tenants, mostly younger white kids fresh out of their parent's house, probably paying rent with their parent's money.

"Jeremy, you there?" I knocked softly to keep the noise down. After a few knocks with no answer I assumed he was asleep. As I walked away frustrated yet relieved the door cracked open.

"Josh, is that you? What are you doin' here this late? Everything OK?"

"Yeah man yeah." He had obviously been asleep but probably not long because once he was out, it was almost impossible to wake him up. I made up a quick lie. "I just left the bar down the street and thought you might be awake. I woke you up though, didn't I?"

"Not really. I was watchin' a movie, just dozin'. Come on in."

"What are you watchin'?"

"I was watchin' *Rush Hour 2* but I guess it's over." The TV screen was completely blue. He plopped back down on the couch. Always messy as a child, Jeremy took pride in cleanliness when he became a young adult, often bursting into sudden cleaning sprees late at night or whenever he was on some type of speed or methadone. At the moment his apartment was dark and dreary with a strong wet sock smell. Clothes, beer bottles and other miscellaneous objects were strewn about the entire apartment. Full ashtrays overflowed with cigarette butts and small pieces of burnt aluminum foil, torn parts of small plastic baggies sat nearby.

"Want a beer?" Jeremy asked as he walked to the kitchen. Following him I noticed an almost empty package of crackers and a bowl of pancake syrup on the counter.

"You eat that?" I asked.

"When it's all I got." He opened the fridge door. Besides half a gallon of milk, a few beers, and ketchup packets, there was nothing.

"Damn, bro. Why don't you spend some of your money on food? I don't see how you live like this."

"Well, I do. I eat out a lot, that's all. I don't let myself go hungry." I knew he was lying. I felt sorry for him, wanted to buy him groceries, but at the same time I knew he wasted his money on drugs.

I sat in the black imitation leather chair and stared at the small TV, the only valuable object in the apartment that had not been pawned. Even his beloved musical instruments were missing. It had been a long time since I had seen him with a guitar in his hand, attempting to learn a new TOOL song or proudly playing one that he had written himself.

Jeremy lit a cigarette. Somehow, he knew I had a reason to be there and quietly waited for me to say something. We both sat silent for a while as I worked up the courage to mention my true motive. Truthfully, my heart begged me to go home or just crash at my brother's, to forget why I was there because only trouble lay ahead. My conscious struggled within me.

"Ya know, I been thinkin'." The words came out fragmented and nervous, hard to get out like on a first date. "I think I'd like to get a little something tonight and try it."

"Whatcha mean?" Jeremy looked at me puzzled but knew exactly what I meant.

"You know, maybe a little tar, just to try it." I tried to use some lingo I had heard from him.

"What? No way. You don't want that stuff. Why you talkin' crazy? You must be drunk or something." He rose up genuinely surprised.

"No, seriously. I don't want to inject it or anything, but maybe to smoke it, to see what it's like."

"Man, I'm not getting you none of that shit. You're just talkin' crazy."

"I'll buy it, enough for both of us. I just want to try it, see what it's like. You're always telling me I can't understand the feeling 'cause I've never done it. Well, I want to."

"You're doin' good in life, Josh. Got a good job, a good girl, nice things. You don't want to do that stuff and ruin it all. Look at me." He waved his hand around showing me the apartment. "Shit, not a day goes by that I wish I hadn't tried it. It's easy to get hooked and just like that, your life can fall to pieces."

"One time won't hurt me. Look at the drugs I did in the past and never got hooked. My personality is not addictive. You know that. C'mon man."

"I can't believe you're really asking me this. I must still be asleep or something. I just can't do it man. I'll feel like shit if somethin' happens to you. What if you like freak out or end up getting hooked? It'll be my fault. I can't deal with that."

"I'm telling you I won't. Is it my fault you're hooked on drugs now 'cause I let you smoke with me when we were younger?"

"No, but still. I just know how powerful this drug is. I'm trying to tell you from experience. It's not so easy just to do it once and then quit. It will take over your life, the craving, the urge. It's like an orgasm times ten, better than sex."

"I doubt that. But if it is, that just gives me another reason to want to try it. Hermano, I just want to see your reality for once. Maybe it'll help me understand your addiction a little. Then I won't be so judgmental and critical all the time."

Jeremy had sat up on the sofa and lit a second cigarette since our conversation had begun. A troubled look of contemplation consumed his demeanor. The thought of getting high with me on a drug like heroin distressed him greatly yet at the same time gave him a personal feeling of satisfaction, fulfilling a long awaited wish. I knew this because I felt exactly the same way. We longed to share every thought, every feeling.

"Look, it's a little late right now. Why don't you come over tomorrow or something and see if you still feel the same way? Maybe you'll be thinking straight and change your mind."

"I've been thinking about this for long time anyway. It's something I want to do. Please. I know you can get it pretty much any time you want. I brought some cash."

It was obviously hard to say no because just the thought of heroin gave Jeremy a craving. Some deep hidden courage made his will temporarily strong when it came to getting me the drug though. The expression on his face had become stern and resolute, like a parent about to give a lecture to his child.

"No. I can't do it. It just doesn't feel right. I don't want to see you end up like me or worse. You're the only strong one in the family, the only one doing right. I respect you for that."

"Fine. I'll find a way to get it on my own then. I just thought it would be better if we could do it together, share the experience. One way or another I'm going to try it." I attempted to be as firm as my brother, stood up, and left the apartment angrily. Probably Jeremy had just prolonged my life but I felt rejected. Tonight I would not enter his world.

XXIII

Our wives prepared the dining room table. Our kids ran around outside playing, so close in age, favorite cousins. The sun was bright, the southern spring air beginning to take effect but not hot yet, the perfect day, the best time of the year. Jeremy and I stood by the flaming grill as we talked, drank a beer, and took turns flipping the burgers. The smell of the cooking meat made us anxious to eat, but as we happily watched our lives in front of us, we could wait.

We talked about nothing in particular, but our faces showed a strong sense of contentment. Time to time we glanced at the children to make sure they hadn't hurt themselves or they weren't destroying anything. Time to time our wives brought us out fresh cold beers and kissed us, both beautiful, both deserving of our love. Then they returned inside while we talked about nothing in particular.

When the burgers were close to ready, we toasted the buns slightly on the grill. Then we brought the large pile of beef inside the house and set it down in the middle of the already prepared table. Ketchup, mayonnaise, mustard, and every other condiment imaginable filled every space available. Crisp, oven-baked French fries sat next to the burgers.

In seconds, the kids rushed the table, opening their Coca Colas and Mountain Dews, grabbing handfuls of fries with their hands still filthy but half-rinsed with water, only because their mothers made them. They piled the fries on the paper plates and splattered ketchup everywhere. Soon, the white tablecloth was stained with a mixture of yellow, red, and other permanent colors. Meanwhile, our wives painstakingly yet lovingly tried to calm the children.

Jeremy and I sat down at opposite ends of the table. We waited to eat while staring at the children and at our wives. Then we looked at each other and smiled. We saw each other's pronounced wrinkles, the few grey hairs beginning to take hold. Not that we looked old, but we realized we were older. A strong sense of pride overcame us. We had made it. We had lived through the tough times and had become older men, happy and content with our place in the world. Most importantly, we were enjoying life together, our families and our future so real and so bright.

Suddenly I heard a loud pounding at the door.

XXIV

The annoying morning knock came to the door surprisingly early. When I opened it, I was even more surprised to see Jeremy standing there. He hesitated to speak but physically he appeared a bit eager.

"You remember coming by last night?" He already knew the answer.

"Of course I do. I barely even had a buzz."

"I can't believe you were really asking me to get heroin for you." He gave a fake laugh and sat down on the couch. "You even called it 'tar'. Where did you hear that?"

"I imagine from you. So what's up?" I replied, exhibiting a pretentious, nonchalant air that bordered on anger, rarely successful with my brother.

"Why are you actin' like that bro? You seriously can't be mad at me for not wanting to buy you dope."

"Well I am. Seriously."

"Damn. I can't believe it. I'm tryin' to look out for you. You don't want any part of this life. Keep what you got, believe me." He sounded deeply sincere, speaking straight from the heart with experience to back it up.

"I heard all this last night. I know what I'm getting into and I was serious. Still am. I'm going to try it one way or another, with or without you."

A look of depressed acquiescence overcame Jeremy's face.

"Look. I've been thinking. I really don't think you should try the stuff but I don't want you to go and do it on your own either. What you said about being able to understand things better and stuff, it's true. There's no way to understand the life of an addict without being part of it. And about you being so judgmental, that's true too. I hate that shit. You're always like that and it bothers me. Maybe trying it *will* help you understand. I'm just scared you might get hooked or something."

"I won't. I don't have that type of personality. So does this mean you'll get us some?"

"You got to promise me this is a one time deal. I'll lose my mind if something happens to you."

"Once or twice, I promise. I want to make sure I really get the affect. I'm a little scared honestly but I'll be fine."

"Promise?"

"Promise."

"OK then. When you want to try it?"

"Now would be cool I guess. I have no plans today."

"So how much do you want?"

"I don't know. Enough for both of us to get a good high. Is fifty dollars enough you think?"

"Plenty. I'll go ahead and call my Mexican friends. They'll hook us up good for fifty. They like me anyway." Jeremy's mood had shifted rather quickly from a reluctant passivity to an enthusiastic zealousness.

Within minutes the transaction was confirmed and we were on the road to Summer Avenue only a few miles from my home. Our destination was an area of town overrun with Hispanics, stores selling chorizo and piñatas, tote-the-note car lots where three or four Mexicans chipped in to buy a cheap vehicle in order to get them to the construction site or the restaurant where they worked.

We waited in a large Autozone parking lot. People paid little or no attention, uncaring or unknowledgeable, oblivious or desensitized to their increasingly degenerate surroundings. A reoccurring daydream passed through my mind in which I had some sort of covert plan to kill the Mexicans that sold dope to

Jeremy. Time and time again I had plotted to secretly kill them or at least destroy their business. I despised them. They gave a bad name to those Latino immigrants who worked tirelessly in the United States trying to earn an honest dollar.

A black, brand new Ford F150 with tinted windows and chromed out rims pulled into the parking lot and slowly cruised towards us.

"That's them. I'll be right back." Jeremy jumped from my car and into the truck when it pulled up next to us.

I stared hard at the two men in the cab hoping to memorize their faces for future reference in case I became man enough to carry out one of my plans. The driver looked my age with a dark clean-shaven face and a bright yellow-collared shirt with the top few buttons undone to expose a thick gold herringbone chain, a stereotypical looking drug dealer. He ignored me while talking with Jeremy. The other stared at me with deep penetrating eyes, the whites bright against his dark face. Also young with a small mustache and long wild hair, he too wore gold. Our eyes remain fixed on each other until Jeremy left the car, almost as if we knew exactly what the other was thinking. As the truck pulled away, we continued to stare, etching each other's face forever in our memory.

"Got it. They hooked us up real good, 'specially since I told 'em this was your first time. We can go back to my crib if you want. I got all the stuff we need already plus we don't have to worry about anybody comin' home. That's what's cool about livin' on your own."

"Sounds good to me." My thoughts about the Mexicans still lingered like a bad aftertaste. Briefly, I had forgotten our purpose and my anger was flaring up. Suddenly I burst out,

"Those mutha fuckers give Mexicans a bad name, you know it? All those people that come here and work their ass off all day to make a living. Then you got these guys wearing big ass gold chains and driving new trucks, probably don't even have real jobs. It makes me sick."

"Damn, bro. What's got into you all of a sudden? Hell, you just gave them fifty bucks."

"I know, I know. But still, it bugs the shit out of me."

"Let's just go to the apartment and chill. Ain't no sense in gettin' worked up about them right now."

"Fine. Let me see what that stuff looks like. I've never seen it for real."

Jeremy pulled what looked like a cut up piece of balloon from his pocket. Inside was a piece of wax paper wrapped around something that resembled a small round pellet of rabbit shit. He stuck out his hand while barely unwrapping the small ball. I stared at it long and hard.

"What the hell is that?" I asked surprised because I felt cheated. "That's what we paid fifty dollars for? There's nothing there but a piece of shit. I thought it was a powder or something."

"It can be. But you snort or shoot the powder most of the time. This is black tar though, what these Mexicans sell. It looks like opium and comes wrapped up in these little balloons and aluminum foil or wax paper so it won't melt. We just bought a fifty dollar balloon."

"That's not any bigger than a freakin' marble."

"It's about four or five good hits a piece. It's enough. I promise you'll feel it."

"So that's is it, huh? I'm gonna smoke a piece of rat shit?" I asked. *"Millions of lives ruined over a small ball of nothing. I should throw it out the fucking window if I know what's good for me."*

"Yep. Just like you heard. Don't look like anything special but it feels great. I put it to my nose to tell if it had a distinct smell.

"Well, like you said, we smoke it right? I won't put a needle in my arm." Just the thought made me nauseous.

"No, that's the powder. You have to mix it with water."

"Yeah, mix it with water and boil it by holding a lighter under a spoon, all that stuff. Hey, I watch TV."

"That's basically it." Jeremy continued in detail about how to smoke heroin, snort it and even shoot it. He seemed almost proud to be teaching me something. I listened intently. There existed a dangerous fascination about the druggie lifestyle that I had never known.

As soon as we arrived to Jeremy's apartment he anxiously jumped out of the car and hurried inside. I was anxious as well, but in a more scared manner.

"It's not too late to back out. Don't do this, don't do this. You'll regret it. You know you will."

He went to his room and noisily ravaged through a few things until he returned with part of an ink pen. The plastic casing was hollowed out and had been cut in half.

One end looked burnt. Obviously it served as a makeshift pipe.

"Come on. Let's get this over with."

"Chill, bro. You're acting like a junkie already and haven't even ever done the stuff." He looked at me as though he could read my mind. "You sure you wanna do this? It ain't too late to say no. I won't think any less of you."

"No. I mean yes. I told you I want to try it. I'm just nervous, that's all. A little scared.

"Don't be. There's nothing to it." As he unwrapped the balloon, he told me the story about his first time.

"You know the first few times I smoked I thought it was opium. I had smoked opium before and that's what it looked like, a small brown ball, sticky. Like you, I thought heroin came in a powder. My friends didn't tell me different."

"Some friends. When did you find out?"

"They eventually told me. Well, here goes. You want the first hit?"

"No, no. I'll watch you." My heart was beating probably faster than it ever had before. We both sat on the couch. Jeremy placed the heroin on the coffee table in front of us. I watched as he lit the small ball and inhaled for what seemed like minutes.

"All you, bro." He handed me the lighter and fell back into the couch blissfully. I mimicked his movements but did not inhale quite as much.

A feeling so difficult to describe engulfed me, one that words can hardly capture. Immediately the smoke seemed to fill my entire body and take control of it, not slowly, but all at once, taking away every concern that I had ever had about life. Nothing mattered. Every bit of anxiety was gone. I simply existed.

"Wow." After a moment of pure serenity and obliviousness I smiled at my brother, now taking his second hit.

"That's what I said my first time." Jeremy chuckled.

Another hit and I lay slowly back on the couch. I didn't care to talk. Fortunately, neither did Jeremy. I wanted to feel the moment. My eyes were closed, the room was silent, and I felt as if someone had wrapped a comfortable warm blanket around me.

XXV

A few weeks passed. Nothing changed. I had tried the evil drug heroin and had liked it. But me, with my type of personality, I wasn't about to become addicted. Only weak-minded fools became slaves to drug use. I had too much to live for. I was too smart and strong-minded.

Life continued, uninterrupted and monotonously normal. As usual, I rarely saw Jeremy and spent most of my time with my girlfriend and preparing for the end of the school year. While she finished nursing school during the summer, I planned to relax and enjoy my vacation. Teaching had its benefits.

Summer arrived, and without a job I had plenty of time on my hands and decided to spend some of it with my brother. We weren't able to frequent bars like I did with other friends or take road trips like in the past because he never had any money. Stealing and selling copper was his only income. Usually we just sat at his apartment watching TV or bootleg movies. Boredom reigned.

"How the hell do you sit here all day and just

watch TV? Doesn't it drive you crazy?"

"Yeah, but I ain't got nothing else to do. Cici's Pizza is supposed to call me back sometime this week. I plan to get as many hours as possible there. They were gonna let me start working last week but I didn't have an ID."

Some new job was always 'supposed' to call him back. A pizza place, a sales position, construction, you name it, he tried it. And in reality he really did attempt to get a job at these places. But without a license (every time he had a state ID he lost it within weeks), without a high school diploma, without transportation, and with a criminal record, no one wanted to hire him.

"Let's go get you a new ID. I'll pay for it and you can pay me back when you start working."

"Are you sure you don't mind? I'll pay ya back my first pay check."

I spent full days driving from place to place, to get an ID, to fill out applications, anything to help him get back on his feet. I could tell that he hated depending on me for everything, but he swallowed his pride. In reality he had no choice and neither did I. He was my brother. More than anything, I cherished the opportunity to spend time together.

We sat on the couch smoking a joint after an early morning of running around the city. Suddenly an urge hit me, like one gets for a certain type of food, perhaps sushi or hot wings, depending on the mood.

"You feel like getting a little tar?" I asked nonchalantly.

"What? Really?" Jeremy looked at me a bit crazy. "Once wasn't enough for you? I know you liked it, but you said you weren't gonna do it again."

"No I didn't. Remember I said I might try it a few times, to get the real effect. Besides, it's been over a month. I don't think doing it again will hurt. I'm bored anyway. Aren't you?"

"Shit, I stay bored. Most of the time that's why I get high. Nothing to do. And then not having a job, that gets me depressed. I hate not working, not being able to do shit. But I can tell you just about every show and actor on television. I should be a fuckin' movie critic or something."

"Fuck it. Let's go get a little then. Call the Mexican."

And so once again we were on our way to Summer Avenue to meet Jeremy's hookup. For some unconscious reason, the inhibition and anxiety that existed my first time had completely disappeared…

XXVI

"You expect me to stick around and watch you do this to yourself? What the hell happened to you? After everything you've seen, everything you've told me, how you would never end up like the rest of your family. Now look at you Josh. You're falling faster than they are. I can't watch you do it, I can't."

She never called me Josh unless she was angry. I could barely make out her words but I remembered how sexy she was when she was angry. Her big brown eyes glared at me, almost ready to cry. I felt so awful and helpless because I knew it was my fault. I hated to hurt her.

"So you're gonna leave me when things get bad, huh? I see how it is." I had nothing else to say in my defense.

"Well do something to get yourself some help! I want to help but you won't let me. Every time I say something you get defensive and so I've kept my mouth shut. But I can't anymore, not when you're coming home everyday fucked up, sleeping all day. When you spend time with me it's like you're not even there. Your

personality has drastically changed, you're broke all the
time, you've lost weight…"

"Damn. You make me sound like a junkie." I
grinned at her.

"You think it's funny? Have you looked in the
mirror lately? That's exactly what you're becoming.
You need help. Fast."

"No, I don't think it's funny." I attempted to hug
her. My movements were sluggish. She pushed me
away.

"No. Don't think you can just make everything
OK with a hug. Please Josh, please get some help. I
love you. I don't want you to ruin your life, our life. I
have so many dreams for us."

"I'm not gettin' any help. I'm fine. School starts
next week and I won't have time to do anything but
work. You don't have to worry."

"Not worry? How can I not worry? The way
you're going you won't be able to go back to work. I'm
going to my mom's. Call me when you can think
straight."

"Bitch!" I yelled as she grabbed her a bag full of
her things and walked out of the door without so much
as a hug or kiss.

Angry and sad at the same time, I began pacing around the house in tears. Rationality was not within my reach at the moment. Thoughts were scattered, distraught. I began throwing lamps, pillows, whatever was within my reach.

"No, no! This can't be fucking happening. I said this would never happen."

I sat down and cried.

"OK. Calm down. Tonight is it. One more time, then I'm done. Tomorrow is a new day. I'll start exercising again. I'll prepare for the new school year. I won't even drink alcohol for a while. I can do it. I know I can. Let me call Jeremy. Just one more time."

"Hey bro. You feel like hangin out? Yeah, Niki's a little pissed. She says I been messed up too much lately. No big deal, she'll get over it. I start school next week so I'll have to quit anyway. What do ya mean? You on her side now? Like you can fuckin' talk. Whatever."

I hung up the phone. Everyone was turning against me. But I didn't need Jeremy either. The number of the Mexicans was saved in my phone. I kept it once after Jeremy called them. Secretly I had met with them a few times but I didn't want anyone to know, not even my brother. If he thought I was getting addicted he might blame himself.

I called the Mexicans. As soon as I hung up I realized that I didn't have a dime on me. My bank account was empty. Already a few nights before I had gathered my change and carried it to a machine at the supermarket that counts it and gives nice, new, crisp bills, but only because I was in a hurry. In the past I would have never done such a thing. Even if it took a long time to count, I would have counted every last cent.

I ransacked the house, searched between the couch cushions, drawers, and in my car. Not a penny was to be found.

"Shit." Nearing a state of frenzy, I looked around the house. "What can I give them? What? I know, how about some CD's?"

I searched through them and tried to pick a few that I might not want to listen to any time soon, but this was taking too long. I had to leave and meet the Mexicans. I grabbed a large stack, as many as I could carry, and walked to the car, leaving the door behind me unlocked. In minutes, I was in an abandoned parking lot awaiting my fix, nervously attempting to arrange the CD's in some type of order.

"Hey Paco. Qué pasa?"

"Nada amigo. Estás bien?

"Yeah but you'll never guess what happened. I thought I had more cash on me but I don't."

"So I give you a smaller bag, no problem. How much you have?"

"That's the thing. I don't have any cash. I brought a shitload of CD's though, good ones, in the original cases and everything."

"CDs? Man, I don't fuckin' trade my shit for CDs. What's wrong with you? You already high?"

"No, no. I just thought, you know, maybe this once…"

"What CD's you have? Let me take look."

"A whole stack. Here." I began to clumsily hand them to him a few at a time. A few fell to the ground on the exchange between car windows. I could feel myself shaking.

"Tranquilo amigo. Necesitas calmarse. What else you have, además los CD's?"

I looked around the car. "Nothing really. Nothing I can think of."

"Tell you what. Mi amigo here needs a car for the night. Has to pick up something very important. Allow him to use it y I give to you the drugs, a nice big balloon. OK?"

"No way man, no way. I can't do that. I won't have a ride home. Something might happen to my car…"

"Está bien. Call me when you have money, OK? But don't bring to me no fuckin' CDs."

"Shit man. All those CDs are worth a lot of money. Can't I get just a little something for them? I'll give them all to you."

"How about I give you real good balloon for the CDs and you car tonight. My friend, he take you home. Drop your car in early morning. Verdad, vato?" He leaned over to his friend and mumbled something under his breath and then looked at me with an evil grin.

"Por supuesto." The other Mexican smiled at me. They were taking full advantage of my vulnerability.

"Damn. Promise he'll bring my car back early in the morning? I've got lots to do tomorrow."

"Ok. No problem."

"What the fuck am I thinking? I can't trust these guys. They keep my car and what do I do? Call the police? 'Yeah, officer, two Mexicans stole my car. I let them have it for the night in exchange for drugs but they

promised to return it first thing in the morning.' They'll bring it back. They will. I know they will. Just keep telling yourself that. Everything will be fine."

The other Mexican jumped into the passenger seat. From past encounters I assumed he spoke little or no English, at least not to me. Probably he was a hired thug, quick to do the bidding of his more intelligent friend. I remembered the first time I had seen him, his wild eyes, his ominous demeanor.

"Qué pasa?" A feigned smile and an attempt to get him to speak triggered no reaction. He stared in a cold, brooding manner as if I was below conversation.

"OK." The ride home was an uncomfortable silence that caused me to regret my decision even more. Still, I continued to drive until I reached the house.

"Look. You're going to take care of this thing, right? I need my vehicle. If something were to happen…" He said nothing and grabbed the keys from my hand. In return he handed me a balloon. It felt like a good size. I wanted to argue or at least get him to offer some sign of affirmation that he would take care of my car.

"So I'll see you in the morning then, right? Early?" He backed out of the driveway with that same intimidating look on his face. I watched the car drive away until it was out of sight and then looked down at the drugs in my hand.

"This better be worth it."

XXVII

"Damn. What time is it?" By the way the sun was shining into my room I knew it had to be late in the afternoon.

"My car!" I attempted to get up quickly to see if the Mexicans had returned my car but my worn body could barely move. The night before had become a blur not long after I had started smoking. I made myself get up.

Peering outside the window I looked for my car. Nothing. My heart dropped. I opened the door and walked outside wearing only my boxer shorts.

"On the street maybe? It's here, it's gotta be here. I just can't see it. Please be here." Nothing. Tears began to well up in my eyes. I approached the street and looked as far as I could in both directions. Nothing.

Inside the house I started screaming and throwing things. I pounded the walls angrily with my fists. Then, after a few minutes of rage, I picked up my cell phone and dialed Paco's number. No answer. Not that I expected one. I dialed again and again.

"Look, this isn't funny. Bring my car back. You said you needed it for the night and I let you use it against my better judgment. Now I need my car." I tried to leave a calm message. If I pissed them off, they might not bring the car back at all.

I paced the house. A few minutes later I called and left another message, this time pleading.

"Listen. Please bring me my car. I really need it. I have so much to do this week."

Only minutes later another,

"Please Paco. I have to have my car. You said you would bring it back in the morning. It's past 4pm now. I'll pay you for the tar. Just bring me my car. Please." Nothing.

In the meantime a few friends called. I refused to answer. As stressed as I felt, surely they would know by my voice that something as wrong. My brother called. *"Maybe he knows something. He talks to those pricks sometimes."*

"Hey bro. What's up?" He seemed in jovial spirits.

"Nothing. Just chillin'."

"You still mad about what I said last night?"

"What did you say?"

"You know, about Niki being right and all. She's just worried about you. Me too a little." The shoe was finally on the other foot. Jeremy was looking out for me.

"I'm fine. *How could I ask him discreetly about the Mexicans?"*

"You sound a little high strung."

"Well, I was just wondering. Have you spoken to the Mexicans today? Or last night?"

"No. Why? I told you I'm not dealing with them anymore. Bro, I'm worried about you. I've never seen you like this before."

"I told you I'm fine. Just let me know if you hear from them or something. I gotta go. Talk to you later."

Within the next half hour I left a few more messages, all polite and pleading, but my patience was thinning. An unfamiliar car pulled up outside and I peered out of the window. Jeremy and a friend got out and made their way to the front door. I locked it quickly and ran to hide in the bedroom. I felt ashamed to confront him at the moment.

"He'll think I'm gone since my car's not here." Suddenly I had a realization.

"Jesus Christ. I bet this is exactly what he used to

do to me. All those times he didn't answer the phone or the door. This is how he felt. He wasn't avoiding me. He was embarrassed. Ashamed." They knocked and knocked and I could hear them talking. Most of the lights in the house were already turned off. Heroin caused an aversion to light. I felt like a fucking vampire.

Eventually they left. What little patience remained in me was gone. I called Paco again and of course, there was no answer.

"Look. I'm through playing. I want my fucking car back or I'll call the police. I know where you hang out, I know your tag number and I know what you look like. I've tried to be nice. I've been a good customer and this is how you treat me? Fuck you. Bring my fucking car back now."

"Shit. I probably shouldn't have done that. Now he'll never bring it back. He may never even call me again. What if I need more tar? No, fuck that. I'm not doing that shit anymore. Look what it's lost me already. My car, my girl. Shit, my sanity. I feel like I'm about to lose my mind."

With no other alternative I lay on the couch and stared blankly at the television. In my mind, a thousand alternate scenes were playing themselves out. Most were violent and ended up with me killing or badly injuring the Mexicans. I would call them and say, "Hey, no hard feelings. Can I still get the hook up?" Then, when we met I would shoot them and take their money and drugs, leaving them dead in the street. Better yet, getting more brutal, I would find out where they lived, go quietly to their homes, and beat them to a bloody pulp. I could imagine all the ways I would torture them, just like in the movies or at Guantanamo Bay. Surely I had a friend or two that would help. Or at least my brother. They would be sorry for coming to America and ruining people's lives and they would especially be sorry for stealing my transportation.

But whom was I kidding? I owned no gun. I didn't have the balls or the will to torture anybody. In actuality I would call the police tomorrow and make up a really great story. Say that I saw some shady looking characters driving by and staring at my house and my car. Say I wrote down their tag number because they looked suspicious. Say I barely saw them but I could tell they were Hispanic.

I practiced the story over and over again to make it more believable. The cops had no reason to suspect me.

I didn't look like a junkie. I had a decent place for a guy my age. I worked. I was respectable, a teacher. They had to believe a teacher. Right?

A soft knock on the door pulled me back to reality. Thinking it might be Jeremy again I peeked surreptitiously out of the window. I still did not want to see anyone. Three Mexicans stood under the dim porch light, two I recognized and another new face. Whatever entered my mind, I knew it was stupid to open the door yet I did it anyway. They walked in with solemn faces and without uttering a word. I immediately knew I was in trouble.

"Hey guys, you made it. I didn't think you …"

A blow to the head knocked me to the ground. The next thing I knew I lay bleeding and covering my face. The two lackeys kicked and threw punches, talking Spanish and spitting on me the whole while. The only words I could make out in the commotion were from Paco, the supposed leader.

"You fuckin' loco talkin' to me like this." He held up his phone and dialed his voice mail. "I answer message and it you telling me to hurry up and bring you car. Sayin' fuck you and all these words I no like."

"Please. I'm sorry. I just wanted my car back.

You promised…"

Every time I looked up or attempted to say something, another fist or foot pounded my body.

"I was going to bring you car but then you talk to me, threaten me. You a crazy gringo. I see people get hooked quick, but you, you like my stuff way too much. And then you say you gonna call the cops? You know me, you know my number? I tell you something. You tell cops or anybody, I come back. I fuckin' kill you. Me entiendes?"

"Yes, yes. I won't tell. I won't tell." I could barely see, my eyes beginning to swell.

"Bueno. And to teach a lesson I keep you car. It teach you not to do heroin. Just say no!" His laugh was deafening, one that would linger with me for the rest of my life. The others laughed as well but probably failed to understand a single word. In seconds, they left just as they entered. The truck engine revved up and the Mexicans disappeared into the night.

My beaten body lay in the floor for an indeterminable amount of time. I wept, more broken in spirit than physically. The darker side of life had taken control. The path I had steered clear of for so long had crept up on me and bit me in the ass. I was a junkie.

And the worse part, all I could think about was getting something to take the pain away.

XXVIII

How quickly life can change with one split second decision. My grandmother once told me the story of a man who wrote to her throughout WWII. He was in love and wanted to marry her. This man's family owned hundreds of acres of land in Colorado. His family had a large ranch with cattle, horses, plenty of money. Colorado means *colored* in Spanish. I've been there, Jeremy and I both. A beautiful place, so picturesque and natural. Better than the boring, flat landscape of the south.

But Grandma married another man, my grandfather, without a bit of regret. He was a good guy, a workingman with little money, but the best that ever walked the earth in her opinion. Everyone loved him. He did no wrong or at least none that anyone remembered. I reminded my grandma of him with my blue eyes, my walk, my entire demeanor.

How different would her life have been if she had married the other man? Would my father, my brother, or I ever existed? She will never know. None of us will ever know the 'other realities', the 'could have beens'.

No, only the present reality exists. Yet so many people dwell on those 'could have been' moments. Often it consumes their thoughts, their actions, their entire lives. They remain full of regret and sorrow and allow all those emotions to control them, attempting to justify why they chose what they chose, why they did what they did, the questions eating away at their sanity. They live in the deep dark past of regret while the present continues to pass away, one miserable day after another.

Not my grandmother. She had no regrets about marrying my grandfather. Almost fifty years together and they were so happy. Now she waits to be with him in heaven.

But my reality is different. A young man and already so many regrets. I hate to look at the past. I used to live for the present. But when the past is all you have and the present is so bleak, what else is there to do? Now I understand. Finally, I understand.

What if my girl would not have had a miscarriage only a few months after we started dating? I would have a two year old now. Imagine. I can't imagine, a two year old. How would that have affected my life? All the things we have done since then. And what if I would have never done drugs with my brother? Would he still have become an addict? And what if I would have never tried heroin? How would my life be now?

XXIX

"How many fucking times will the phone ring?"
My entire body ached. I could feel myself getting sick.
The last thing I wanted was somebody asking me how I
was doing. I refused to answer the phone and the door.
I stopped counting the number of times someone had
called or came by the house. Sooner or later they would
break the door down or call the police to rescue me. The
only reason they probably had not already done so was
because my car was gone. Forever.

Before the pain got too bad, I thought I could walk
a couple of miles to the area near my old apartment.
There were plenty of dealers standing on the corners,
especially on warm weekend nights. I had never bought
drugs from them, but on more than one occasion they
had said to me,

"Man, whatever you need I got it. Want some
yams? Got 'em. Herb? Got it? Want your dick
sucked? I can do that."

I hated living so close to such a degenerate part of
society but the rent was cheap and the Midtown area
was the only place in Memphis that had a somewhat

vibrant, eclectic atmosphere. Besides, I ignored the dealers and junkies, so long as they didn't wander too close to our apartment.

"But what do I have to give them?" I asked myself looking around the room. My CD's were mostly gone. Some remained, as well as some DVD's and the DVD player. I could carry those for a distance. I put them in a white plastic Wal-Mart bag and began to get dressed. As soon as I was ready to walk out of the door my brother pulled up as if he had been waiting and watching the house. It was too late to avoid him.

"Where you been?" I returned inside and set the bag down. I kept my head lowered.

"What the hell happened to you?" He exclaimed after seeing the cuts and bruises on my face.

"Nothing."

"Nothing. What do you mean nothing? Look at your face. It's fucked up." He tried to get a good look. "And your car. Where is it? I've stopped by a few times and haven't seen it. Thought you were gone."

"I got in a wreck. My car's totaled. Hopefully the insurance will pay but it was my fault, and uh, I only had liability."

"Really?" He asked condescendingly. He knew I

was lying.

"So where are you heading now? I saw you leaving and carrying that bag in the floor with you." He walked over to the bag and attempted to pick it up. I pushed him before he reached it.

"It's none of your goddamn business where I'm going! What the hell is your problem? Since when are you my daddy?"

"Chill bro. You seem to have the problem. I see what's in the bag. Your DVDs and the DVD player. You going to sell them?"

"Maybe. I got no car and no money. What else can I do?"

"No money? What do you need money for?"

"Food."

"You got a job, right? Don't you get paid during the summer?"

"Yes, but only once a month. I've done spent it all though. Anyway, why don't you ask your friend to give me a ride to the pawn shop?"

"Are you crazy? It closed man. It's almost 10pm on a Saturday night. If you want, you can come to my apartment and eat. I got some food. Shit, we'll order a pizza and watch some movies or something. I'll pay."

"No. I think I'm just gonna chill here. I ate not too long ago. I can wait until tomorrow. Plus I'm a little tired."

"And what tomorrow? The pawnshops are still closed. C'mon man. Come over to my place. I'm worried about you."

"I don't feel like going anywhere, didn't you fuckin' hear me? Shit, leave me alone." I felt increasingly irritated.

"Bro, don't act like this. It's just the drugs talking. You're edgy and about to go through withdrawals. It's gonna hurt man. I know. I've been there. Looking at you is like looking into a mirror right now. I'll help you get through it."

"I'm not going through anything. I've just had a bad week, that's all. I start school on Monday and everything will be fine."

"This Monday? Shit, I don't think you're gonna be ready by Monday. Even if you could, how are you gonna get there?" The thought had not crossed my mind.

"I don't know. I haven't thought about it." My mind felt so scattered and clouded. Reason told me I was in a predicament and needed to get out. The only way to do this would be to give in to Jeremy and not get any more drugs. Go to his house and let him take care of me while I went through withdrawals. I could feel the pain coming on. But even afterwards, I doubted I would be in any shape to make it to school on Monday. I had realized this for a while really, but never wanted to admit it.

The other side of my mind pulled stronger. It told me to hurry up and appease my hunger, my rapacious need. It didn't want to go through any type of pain. It wanted my body to feel good, if only for a brief period. The urge was overwhelming.

"Bro. You still with me? C'mon man, let's get out of here and go to my crib. You'll be OK."

"No! Get the fuck out of here! I told you I'm fine. I'm not sick, I'm not going through nothing. I'll be fine. Just get out!"

"Josh, we're all worried about you. Mom and dad, grandma, they been calling, trying to get a ride up here to see you. Please..."

"Fuck them. They should have worried about us years ago when we were their responsibility. Pieces of shit. I'm tired of putting up with them. I would have left this shitty city years ago if not for them. You too.

We could have been in California right now, just like we've promised ourselves so many times. But no, where are we?"

"I know bro, I know. And we can still go. It's never too late. Never. I know mom and dad are messed up, but they love us. They're not keeping us from going anywhere. If anything, it's the drugs."

"Whatever. I don't want to hear this shit right now. Please just get out and leave me alone. I'll be fine. I'm tired. I want to lay down." I walked towards my room.

"Ok. But promise me you'll stay here at the house and won't go anywhere tonight." I felt like a child.

"Ok. I promise."

"And call me if you change your mind. I'll be back to check on you first thing tomorrow morning. I'm not gonna let you do this on your own."

"Fine. I'll be here."

"Alright. I love you bro. See you tomorrow, right?" His eyes were so caring. It was difficult to lie.

"Fine. See you. And tell mom and dad I'm fine too. And don't tell them what I said OK? Or about the wreck. I don't want them worried about me."

"I won't. But you didn't really have a wreck, did

you?"

I hesitated and confessed.

"No."

"We'll get those Mexicans. I owe them one myself. Take care bro. See you tomorrow. Remember, call me if you need anything."

"See you." I shut the bedroom door, lay down in bed, and waited a good five minutes until the sounds faded. Not having the patience to wait any longer, I got up from the bed and returned to the living room. I grabbed the bag and before I left, I walked around the house to see if there was anything else to take. I put my cell phone in my pocket. Finally, I jammed the laptop, my most prized possession and the most expensive thing I owned, into the already about-to-bust bag. It was almost a week before I returned home.

XXX

"My stomach. Haven't taken a shit in almost a week. Can't believe it. Tried drinking coffee, anything that will help me shit."

The house was almost empty save a few dishes, a lamp, and the dope addicts that I allowed to stay there on the condition they kept me high. Since it was only a matter of time before the landlord came to evict me, I had gotten rid of everything worth selling. Rent was two months behind, maybe more. My sense of time had slipped away some time ago.

"Hey, you OK? You look like you're about to bust." Demetrius hovered over me as I sat in a balled up position on the floor clutching my stomach. He appeared to be the only coherent and alert person in the room.

"My stomach is killing me, man. I haven't eaten in I don't know when but even if I wanted to I don't think I could."

"I got some chips in the kitchen. Maybe an apple or two."

"Not right now. Maybe later."

"Well, you want me to fix you up? Got some really good stuff this go round." Demetrius was my brother's age, maybe a year or two younger. He made money in any manner possible, a young entrepreneur as he called himself. Drugs appeared to be the most profitable. Not only had he purchased most of my possessions or traded them for drugs, he had taken control of my bedroom where there still remained a few things – a mattress, some of my clothing, and a small television. Meanwhile, I slept on a blanket in the living room on the uncomfortable hardwood floor.

I stared around the near empty room. A younger girl who looked barely out of high school sat in the corner. She was pretty, but signs that the beauty was quickly fading away were obvious. Her head lay limp on the shoulder of a guy who appeared a few years older and farther from redemption. He had probably pulled her down with him. Still another lifeless body lay covered up with a blanket. He had made himself a permanent piece of furniture in the house. I vaguely remembered smoking with him a time or two.

"What ya got?" I asked.

"Got some Dilaudid."

"Sure. Why not?" It really didn't matter anymore

what drug I took, so long as I stayed high. Everyone had a drug of choice, but a true addict took anything that got him high. We rarely discriminated. By now, I had tried almost everything. I preferred the downers, the stuff that numbed me, took away all sense of my surroundings, all my problems. Crack was the easiest and cheapest to get so that's what we did the most. But the high didn't last long and always made me eager for more.

"You got a tool handy?" I held out my right arm. Tracks covered it. I remembered Niki always wanting to practice giving me IVs while she attended nursing school.

"You've got the perfect veins," she told me. "Why don't you let me practice on them? I can give a great IV."

"Hell no. I believe you. I hate needles. I could never shoot up. I don't see how people do it."

Never had I given myself an injection. I just let whoever seemed the most functional at the time do it while my eyes remained closed. The first time was scary, but afterwards the warm feeling took all anxiety away, so relieving. It hit so much quicker than smoking or snorting, ran through my whole body instantaneously.

Demetrius prepared the syringe. No sooner did I have my eyes closed and felt the tip of the needle touching my arm than we heard the sound of a key. The door swung open. The landlord walked in.

"What the… What the hell are you all doing here? What's going on? Get out! Now! I'm calling the police." His facial expression was first one of confusion and surprise but quickly changed to rage once he became aware of the situation.

"This is why you can't pay rent, huh? No wonder." He walked toward me as I clumsily tried to get to my feet. Demetrius intervened and got in his face. Maybe the landlord owned the house, but with a six-foot plus black guy in his personal space he thought twice about causing a scene.

"Chill, old man. This your pad?

"Yes it is. And you all need to leave immediately." The landlord fumbled around in his pocket for a cell phone. He adjusted his glasses. A drop of sweat formed on his brow.

"How much you want to rent this place?" Demetrius attempted to mediate the situation.

"Somebody else has already rented it. That's why I'm here. Listen now, I'm calling the cops."

"Yeah, yeah, I heard ya. If you know what's good for ya, you'll wait till I leave." His face was an inch or less from the landlord's.

"I don't want trouble. Josh was supposed to be out of here over a month ago. I just came by to make sure the place was empty and I find... I find all this." He looked around disgusted and shook his head as if he had never seen such a sight.

"Ok. I'm gonna grab my stuff and I'm gone. But don't call the cops, not till I leave. You hear me?"

"Sure, sure." Demetrius went to the bedroom. We could hear him rummaging through things. I looked around to see if there was anything I could take with me. I grabbed a blanket. The people passed out on the floor I didn't really know so I didn't bother waking them. They probably would not have moved anyway.

"This house is a piece of shit anyway. I don't know how many times I called you to fix something." It was a bad attempt at justifying the situation.

"Just get out. Now." He stood holding the door open.

Leaving the bodies on the cold hardwood, Demetrius and I left. The police would take care of them.

"Got my car hidden a few blocks away for precisely this reason." Demetrius was pissed.

"Prepared like a boy scout aren't you?" I tried to make the best of the situation but in truth any emotion I had was completely numbed.

"Got to be. Dealin' with junkies like you. You told me rent was paid up and we didn't havta worry bout shit."

"That was like a month ago. You know I haven't had the money to pay."

"Yeah, yeah. Well, the law will probably be lookin' for us soon. That old crazy cracker, dressed up in his suit an' shit. I was about to pop his ass, especially if he woulda called the cops. He looked scared didn't he?" Demetrius laughed arrogantly.

"Yeah, he did. Dude's a dick. I don't mind screwin' him over really. He was supposed to fix a lot of shit around there but he never did. What about the others that we left there? They'll go to jail for sure."

"Oh well. Not my problem. Once you junkies get hooked ya'll forget everything in life except the drugs. Don't nothin' else matter. I will sure miss hittin' that cute little white girl though."

"What? You been with her? How long has she

been there?"

"Couple a weeks on and off. Her boyfriend brought her over, got her hooked."

"And he don't care if you're bangin' her?"

"Mind? Man, he be watchin'. I done brought my boys over and everything, we be nuttin' in her face three at a time, all in front of him. He's been pimpin' her out for drugs."

"Damn. And she don't mind? What is she, like sixteen?"

"Of course she don't mind. Once you go black you never go back. And I hope she's at least eighteen though. Who knows? I think she's a runaway. Here's my ride. What you gonna do?"

"I was thinking I could go with you, maybe at least for a couple of days until I figure out where to go."

"Man, I can't be taking you with me. I gots to go to my auntie's or somewhere safe for a few days. You know the cops will be lookin' for us. Why don't you go stay with your brother or somethin'? Get a shower. You need one."

"No. Not my family. They can't see me right now. Not until I can get back on my feet."

"Well, I'm gone. Maybe I'll see you later on

down the road."

"Can you at least drop me at the park?"

"The park?" Shit, I guess. Get in." Overton Park
was a few streets over. On the way, two cops cars
passed us. We both turned around.

"How about that Dilatad before I leave?"

"Man, you pushin' your luck ain't you?

"C'mon man. You've been stayin' at my house
for weeks now."

"And I been supplyin' your drug habit too." He
reached in his pocket of pants that were too large for
him. "Here, here's $10. Now get out of my car. Get
yourself together."

"Ok. Take care Demetrius."

"Yeah, you too. Later."

And so on a pleasant autumn afternoon I found a
temporary home in the park. I walked around and
listened to the wind in the trees. Though still a bit
sluggish and drowsy, my stomachache was gone. I felt
better than I had in a long while. Being outside
surrounded by nature and away from dealers and junkies
felt liberating. Even more liberating was the feeling of
freedom: freedom from owing landlords, freedom from
possessions, especially since I had none, and freedom

from the problems of family and friends. For the first time of my life I felt like a man liberated from the chains of civilization, without obligation and responsibility, just as I had always wanted to be.

"Maybe this is an opportunity to start over. I can travel around from place to place. Do odd jobs, hitchhike, maybe join the Rainbow Family. Other people do it. I've seen them. Why can't I? This is what I've always wanted. An excuse to escape. A chance to see the country. A chance to be like Jack Kerouac in 'On the Road'.

Perhaps it took a major downfall for me to reach this point, but my mind was at rest. I contemplated how I would begin. I could start by walking to the interstate and getting out of Memphis. That alone would be an amazing accomplishment. I felt resentment towards the city, as if it was culpable for my many problems.

The comfortable breeze kept me daydreaming most of the day. As the sun was setting I promised it would be the last I would watch in this godforsaken place. The southern sunset was in truth one of the most beautiful I had ever witnessed. No one could take that away. A flood of memories came rushing back to me. I still had $10 in my pocket.

XXXI

"It's like an orgasm times ten, better than sex. Or how about the saying 'it's like being kissed by god." Those words were unbelievable at another time and place, seemingly impossible. *"What could be better than sex? What? Females, I love females. Too bad they don't tell you that the libido is pretty much fucking dead when you're an addict. Fuck sex, heroin is all I need. It's not like X or alcohol that drops your inhibitions and gets you ready to fuck. Nope. It's evil. It takes away all that is natural.*

My girl. She's gone, left me. Yeah. Can't blame her. Nope. I can blame her, fuck her, bitch. A girl who says she loves you. Wants to be your wife, she's supposed to stick with you through thick and thin. I loved her. Never cheated on her. Promised myself I wouldn't. But she left anyway. Says she couldn't stand to see me kill myself. Probably with another dude by now. So it's me, just me. All an individual ever really has in the world is his own self.

It's cold out tonight. Mind racing a hundred miles an hour. Can't think straight, never able to think straight. Damn weather around here changes so much, cold one minute, hot the next. What's that saying? If you don't like the weather in Memphis, wait a few minutes, it'll change. Something like that. Yeah. See, I can remember some things. What am I doing out here this late anyway? Already high. It'll wear off soon. Too soon. Money, I need money. Drugs, I need drugs. Yeah. Gotta get the money to get the drugs. Hope someone stops by soon, needs a hookup, a blowjob, sex, anything to help me get high.

Never thought it would come to this. Used to wonder about Jeremy. Wonder if he ever did this. Never asked. He'd lie anyway. I'd lie. Doesn't matter anymore. Don't ever see anyone I know. Done fucked them all over, burned my bridges. Fuckers weren't my friends anyway.

Used to live nearby here. Knew what was going on even then. 'How fuckin' nasty,' I'd think to myself. 'Fuckers need to be killed. Fuckin' fags and dope addicts.' But drugs, drugs do it all, responsible for everything, ruinin' families, destroying lives, making people do messed up things and sink to a primordial level. Crazy.

Look at me. I'm a piece of shit now. Shit. I hate

myself. I wish I would have never.... I can still stop. I just wanted to be close to my brother, to understand him. I'm still young. Maybe tomorrow I'll change. No. Can't. Just want to fuckin' die. Been through too much. Life wasn't supposed to be this tough.

There's a pair of lights driving slow. Let me step out so they can see me. Here they come. Here they come. Yeah, they're goin' to stop."

"Hey man. Can I help you with something tonight?" A man behind a tinted window rolled down to get a good look.

"Sure. Want to get in the car?"

"I can do that."

In the driver's seat of a newer model mustang a middle-aged white man smiled and rolled the windows back up.

"I can pretty much get whatever you need. I'm you're guy."

"Oh I've already got what I need. In fact, I'm willing to share a little bit of what I got with you if you can give me what I want." The man rubbed his crotch.

"Yeah, Ok. Depends on what you got though."

"Try a little bit of this." He took a small keyful of yellow powder from an envelope and held it to my nose.

"Fuck yeah. Damn." It burnt badly but didn't keep me from doing another.

"There's plenty more where that come from."

"Great." I reached for the bag.

"Whoa now, soldier. Hold up. You don't think I'm going to give away this high quality stuff for free do you? I want something in return."

"Ok, Ok." Already I could feel the drugs running through my body, my heart racing.

"I'm going to drive over to where it's a little darker and no one can see us. How's that?"

"Sure, sure. Whatever. How about another bump?"

"In a minute." He drove the vehicle to a secluded wooded area without illumination. I dreaded where the situation was leading but I needed the high.

"This ought to do." He turned off the ignition but left the keys inside. "Alright. I think you know what I want."

"I need another bump first, man. Something to get me through this shit."

"Yeah, yeah, whatever. One more. The better you do, the more I'll give ya."

The next few minutes were disgusting. My mind

tried to it block out. Now there was no turning back. I had sunk as low on the scale of human existence as possible. *"I wish I was dead."*

"Yeah, that's right. A little slower. You like that don't you. I bet you dream of me for the rest of the night and hope I come back."

I was getting sick to my stomach. *"Please hurry up,"* I thought to myself. And here he was, asking me to go slower.

"Think of something else. Happy thoughts. Traveling. Those years of teaching. How happy I used to be. Riding bikes through this same park with my girlfriend."

"Fuck yeah!" He pushed my head hard to the side and it hit the gearshift. "God that was great. You're just a little fuckin' pro, aren't you? Bet you've done this before."

"No, not really. I just need some money, some drugs, something to keep me going. Been through some bad times lately. I ..."

"Shut the fuck up. I don't want to hear your pitiful stories. You're a fucking junkie, sucking dick to get high. But hey, thank god you're out here on a cold night like this. I was needing a nut. Now get the fuck out of my car."

"Man, you told me you were gonna give me something in return. I'm not getting out till I get it."

"Feisty little thing aren't you. Maybe it was that stuff I gave ya. It does that." I wanted to kill this faggot, dressed up like a wannabe model from GQ with massive amounts of hair gel and cologne.

"Well, you sure as hell didn't give me enough for what I did."

"Ok, Ok. You ungrateful little shit. That was my good stuff but I've got something else you'll like almost as good." He reached into the glove compartment and grabbed a plastic baggie containing white powder. "Do you have something to hold part of this?"

I searched my pockets. I noticed the cellophane around his cigarette pack.

"Can I use that?"

"Sure, why not. I just want to hurry up and get the fuck out of here."

He put quite a bit of the powder into the wrapper. I didn't ask what was inside but from experience I thought it might be crystal meth.

"Ok. Out." Dude was an asshole. But who respects a junkie?

I opened the door and before both feet were on the ground he sped away. I caught myself before I fell but scraped my hand.

"Asshole!" I looked around for something to throw but my thoughts immediately shifted back to my new baggie full of powder. I searched for a peaceful area in the nearby woods, away from the view of people or the traffic from the main street. An open, moonlit spot on the ground called my name. Within seconds I was doing line after line, almost as if I had a death wish. I had never felt so shameful, so dirty and despicable. If I would have had a gun I would have already been dead. I lay the baggie down next to me.

"Damn, hold up. Don't feel right. Heart racing. Am I about to have an overdose? A heart attack? Good. No, wait a minute. I'm not ready to die. I'm so young. Maybe this will be a wake-up call. I mean, people live through these things right? My mom did. Jeremy tells me stories of his friends who have. Fuck. Feel so strange. Body and mind separated, not in sync, not wanting to collaborate. Pass out. Do something. Getting numb. Wait. Where the fuck am I? In the park? Yes, but hiding in the woods. How will anybody ever find me in time? Maybe if I walk out to the street.

No. Can't move. Can't function. Never felt like this. Oh God. I'm so sorry. Never meant to be like this. I was good for most of my life, right? Does that count? It's not my fault. You're the one who created this evil that man has no control over. So many just like me. Good souls deep down. Addicted, weak, but still good deep down. All I ever wanted was to understand...

XXXII

"Thought I'd be the first to go. I've been doing drugs since I was fourteen years old. Here I am, twenty-eight and still alive. Sure, I've got plenty of problems. Living with my mom, making minimum wage at a dead end job. No girlfriend, no car, no money. But hey, I'm alive.

Maybe Josh got out the easy way. He didn't experience all the withdrawals, the pain he caused others, the slow deterioration of his body at such a young age. Drugs take a toll. He lived a good life for the most part. Had it made. A good job, a beautiful girl. I envied him. Envied him since I was a little kid. My whole life basically.

My parents look so pitiful over there, standing at the casket, tears in their eyes. Never seen them so sad. Parents are supposed to go before their kids. That's just the natural order of things. I can't get close. I hate funerals. But this funeral... I can't get close. I'll go crazy, fucking crazy. My brother, my big brother. Gone forever.

It's my fault he tried that stuff. No it's not. Yes it is. He would tell me it's not but I hooked him up the first few times. That's enough. My fault. Had no idea he was getting so bad. How could I? He always acted so strong, never told anyone his problems. Not me, not my parents. He was too strong. Tried to be strong for everyone in the family. What a load to bear. Not strong enough though. Finally broke down. I really thought he could do it without getting addicted. 'Just once', he told me. 'Just once. I want to understand.' He was strong. Not strong enough though."

"Jeremy, aren't you going to come see your brother." My mother could barely get the words out. I wanted to be strong. I wanted to be by her side and let her cry on my shoulder but I couldn't get close.

"That's not Josh momma. Josh is someplace better."

The words made her cry as she tried to smile at me.

"You're right baby boy, you're right."

Father understood why I couldn't get close. He came and hugged me tightly. I cried into his chest. The pain was unbearable.

"Always thought he would live longer..."

XXXIII

"Peering down into the canyon, I know the terrain will take care of me. It's deep enough without many rocks in the way. This spot is the best I've found. Driven around all day. Driven around to several spots, some two or three times. Gotta find the best spot, the least painful, the most beautiful. This is the spot where Josh and I sat and watched the sunset. Man I miss him.

Silently, with lips closed, I speak to Josh. We wait for the many tourists to depart. We want nothing more than to do this alone. He tells me to be patient. 'Time is on our side,' he says. "But it hurts. I'm ready for the pain to go away," I tell him. 'It will. I promise.'

The sunset is the most magnificent I have ever seen, a sky painted fire orange by the sun and streaked with a hundred shades of blue. Its light transforms the canyon into something magical, something spiritual. Its beauty is a sign, a sign calling me back home.

No matter how benevolent the sunset appears, nothing can make me feel whole again, nothing can fill the void. My plight on this earth is finished. Life was tough before, but now, it's pointless. Without family, what do I have?

Josh keeps talking to me. People in my family who have died always talk to me. My grandpa, my uncle, now my brother. They tell me they are with me, they are watching over me and I know it's true. Soon I will be with them.

The tourists don't want to leave. I see them watching out of the corner of their eye. Maybe they suspect something. Why don't they try to stop me? Why don't they just hurry up and go away.

I've always been impatient, always wanted everything in a hurry, right now, at this moment. Josh always told me to be patient, to calm down. Now I'm being patient, when it's too late, when it doesn't matter. No. It matters. Gotta do this right.

The sun is gone. I think the tourists will be gone soon, only a few left. There they go now, off in their cars to their campsites with their family. With their family. Family. Family.

It's time. Quiet. All I hear are the insects. Probably the insects will be the first to find me. All night my body will lay there bleeding and broken. Hope I die quickly. I made sure it was a long way down. No way to live through it.

How long will my body be there? Will the coyotes find it? Mountain lions? Vultures? Even if people look down in daylight they might not see me. But my body isn't important. My soul, my soul is what matters. My soul is what will be with my family soon, what will continue on and on forever.

One last look over the edge. Can't really see anything in the dark. I've seen it enough, been here almost all day. Only one thing left to do..."

TWO BROTHERS